THE
RED CROSS GIRL

Richard Harding Davis

With An Introduction By Gouverneur Morris

1st WORLD
LIBRARY
Literary Society

The Red Cross Girl

Richard Harding Davis

© 1st World Library – Literary Society, 2004
PO Box 2211
Fairfield, IA 52556
www.1stworldlibrary.org
First Edition

LCCN: 2004091269

Softcover ISBN: 1-59540-687-5
eBook ISBN: 1-59540-787-1

Purchase *"The Red Cross Girl"*
as a traditional bound book at:
www.1stWorldLibrary.org/purchase.asp?ISBN=1-59540-687-5

1st World Library Literary Society is a nonprofit organization dedicated to promoting literacy by:

- Creating a free internet library accessible from any computer worldwide.
- Hosting writing competitions and offering book publishing scholarships.

Readers interested in supporting literacy through sponsorship, donations or membership please contact:
literacy@1stworldlibrary.org
Check us out at: www.1stworldlibrary.org

The Red Cross Girl
contributed by the Charles Family
in support of
1st World Library Literary Society

CONTENTS

INTRODUCTION

R. H. D.

"And they rise to their feet as he passes, gentlemen unafraid."

He was almost too good to be true. In addition, the gods loved him, and so he had to die young. Some people think that a man of fifty-two is middle-aged. But if R. H. D. had lived to be a hundred, he would never have grown old. It is not generally known that the name of his other brother was Peter Pan.

Within the year we have played at pirates together, at the taking of sperm whales; and we have ransacked the Westchester Hills for gunsites against the Mexican invasion. And we have made lists of guns, and medicines, and tinned things, in case we should ever happen to go elephant shooting in Africa. But we weren't going to hurt the elephants. Once R. H. D. shot a hippopotamus and he was always ashamed and sorry. I think he never killed anything else. He wasn't that kind of a sportsman. Of hunting, as of many other things, he has said the last word. Do you remember the Happy Hunting Ground in "The Bar Sinister"? - "Where nobody hunts us, and there is nothing to hunt."

Experienced persons tell us that a man-hunt is the most

exciting of all sports. R. H. D. hunted men in Cuba. He hunted for wounded men who were out in front of the trenches and still under fire, and found some of them and brought them in. The Rough Riders didn't make him an honorary member of their regiment just because he was charming and a faithful friend, but largely because they were a lot of daredevils and he was another.

To hear him talk you wouldn't have thought that he had ever done a brave thing in his life. He talked a great deal, and he talked even better than he wrote (at his best he wrote like an angel), but I have dusted every corner of my memory and cannot recall any story of his in which he played a heroic or successful part. Always he was running at top speed, or hiding behind a tree, or lying face down in a foot of water (for hours!) so as not to be seen. Always he was getting the worst of it. But about the other fellows he told the whole truth with lightning flashes of wit and character building and admiration or contempt. Until the invention of moving pictures the world had nothing in the least like his talk. His eye had photographed, his mind had developed and prepared the slides, his words sent the light through them, and lo and behold, they were reproduced on the screen of your own mind, exact in drawing and color. With the written word or the spoken word he was the greatest recorder and reporter of things that he had seen of any man, perhaps, that ever lived. The history of the last thirty years, its manners and customs and its leading events and inventions, cannot be written truthfully without reference to the records which he has left, to his special articles and to his letters. Read over again the Queen's Jubilee, the Czar's Coronation, the March of the Germans through Brussels, and see for yourself if I speak too zealously, even for a friend, to whom, now that R. H. D. is dead, the world can never be the same again.

But I did not set out to estimate his genius. That matter will come in due time before the unerring tribunal of posterity.

One secret of Mr. Roosevelt's hold upon those who come into contact with him is his energy. Retaining enough for his own use (he uses a good deal, because every day he does the work of five or six men), he distributes the inexhaustible remainder among those who most need it. Men go to him tired and discouraged, he sends them away glad to be alive, still gladder that he is alive, and ready to fight the devil himself in a good cause. Upon his friends R. H. D. had the same effect. And it was not only in proximity that he could distribute energy, but from afar, by letter and cable. He had some intuitive way of knowing just when you were slipping into a slough of laziness and discouragement. And at such times he either appeared suddenly upon the scene, or there came a boy on a bicycle, with a yellow envelope and a book to sign, or the postman in his buggy, or the telephone rang and from the receiver there poured into you affection and encouragement.

But the great times, of course, were when he came in person, and the temperature of the house, which a moment before had been too hot or too cold, became just right, and a sense of cheerfulness and well-being invaded the hearts of the master and the mistress and of the servants in the house and in the yard. And the older daughter ran to him, and the baby, who had been fretting because nobody would give her a double-barrelled shotgun , climbed upon his knee and forgot all about the disappointments of this uncompromising world.

He was touchingly sweet with children. I think he was a little afraid of them. He was afraid perhaps that they wouldn't find out how much he loved them. But when they showed him that they trusted him, and, unsolicited, climbed upon him and laid their cheeks against his, then the loveliest expression came over his face, and you knew that the great heart, which the other day ceased to beat, throbbed with an exquisite bliss, akin to anguish.

One of the happiest days I remember was when I and mine received a telegram saying that he had a baby of his own. And I thank God that little Miss Hope is too young to know what an appalling loss she has suffered....

Perhaps he stayed to dine. Then perhaps the older daughter was allowed to sit up an extra half-hour so that she could wait on the table (and though I say it, that shouldn't, she could do this beautifully, with dignity and without giggling), and perhaps the dinner was good, or R. H. D. thought it was, and in that event he must abandon his place and storm the kitchen to tell the cook all about it. Perhaps the gardener was taking life easy on the kitchen porch. He, too, came in for praise. R. H. D. had never seen our Japanese iris so beautiful; as for his, they wouldn't grow at all. It wasn't the iris, it was the man behind the iris. And then back he would come to us, with a wonderful story of his adventures in the pantry on his way to the kitchen, and leaving behind him a cook to whom there had been issued a new lease of life, and a gardener who blushed and smiled in the darkness under the Actinidia vines.

It was in our little house at Aiken, in South Carolina, that he was with us most and we learned to know him best, and that he and I became dependent upon each other in many ways.

Events, into which I shall not go, had made his life very difficult and complicated. And he who had given so much friendship to so many people needed a little friendship in return, and perhaps, too, he needed for a time to live in a house whose master and mistress loved each other, and where there were children. Before he came that first year our house had no name. Now it is called "Let's Pretend."

Now the chimney in the living-room draws, but in those first days of the built-over house it didn't. At least, it didn't draw all the time, but we pretended that it did, and with much pretense came faith. From the fireplace that smoked to the serious things of life we extended our pretendings, until real troubles went down before them - down and out.

It was one of Aiken's very best winters, and the earliest spring I ever lived anywhere. R. H. D. came shortly after Christmas. The spireas were in bloom, and the monthly roses; you could always find a sweet violet or two somewhere in the yard; here and there splotches of deep pink against gray cabin walls proved that precocious peach-trees were in bloom. It never rained. At night it was cold enough for fires. In the middle of the day it was hot. The wind never blew, and every morning we had a four for tennis and every afternoon we rode in the woods. And every night we sat in front of the fire (that didn't smoke because of pretending) and talked until the next morning.

He was one of those rarely gifted men who find their chiefest pleasure not in looking backward or forward, but in what is going on at the moment. Weeks did not have to pass before it was forced upon his knowledge that Tuesday, the fourteenth (let us say), had been a good Tuesday. He knew it the moment he waked at 7 A. M. and perceived the Tuesday sunshine making patterns of bright light upon the floor. The sunshine rejoiced him and the knowledge that even before breakfast there was vouchsafed to him a whole hour of life. That day began with attentions to his physical well-being. There were exercises conducted with great vigor and rejoicing, followed by a tub, artesian cold, and a loud and joyous singing of ballads.

At fifty R. H. D. might have posed to some Praxiteles and, copied in marble, gone down the ages as "statue of a young athlete." He stood six feet and over, straight as a Sioux chief, a noble and leonine head carried by a splendid torso. His skin was as fine and clean as a child's. He weighed nearly two hundred pounds and had no fat on him. He was the weight-throwing rather than the running type of athlete, but so tenaciously had he clung to the suppleness of his adolescent days that he could stand stiff-legged and lay his hands flat upon the floor.

The singing over, silence reigned. But if you had listened at his door you must have heard a pen going, swiftly and boldly. He was hard at work, doing unto others what others had done unto him. You were a stranger to him; some magazine had accepted a story that you had written and published it. R. H. D. had found something to like and admire in that story (very little perhaps), and it was his duty and pleasure to tell you so. If he had liked the story very much he would send you instead of a note a telegram. Or it might be that you had drawn a picture, or, as a cub reporter, had shown golden promise in a half column of unsigned print, R. H. D. would find you out, and find time to praise you and help you. So it was that when he emerged from his room at sharp eight o'clock, he was wide-awake and happy and hungry, and whistled and double-shuffled with his feet, out of excessive energy, and carried in his hands a whole sheaf of notes and letters and telegrams.

Breakfast with him was not the usual American breakfast, a sullen, dyspeptic gathering of persons who only the night before had rejoiced in each other's society. With him it was the time when the mind is, or ought to be, at its best, the body at its freshest and hungriest. Discussions of the latest plays and novels, the doings and undoings of statesmen, laughter and sentiment - to him, at breakfast, these things were as important as sausages and thick cream.

Breakfast over, there was no dawdling and putting off of the day's work (else how, at eleven sharp, could tennis be played with a free conscience?). Loving, as he did, everything connected with a newspaper, he would now pass by those on the hall-table with never so much as a wistful glance, and hurry to his workroom.

He wrote sitting down. He wrote standing up. And, almost you may say, he wrote walking up and down. Some people, accustomed to the delicious ease and clarity of his style, imagine that he wrote very easily. He did and he didn't. Letters, easy, clear, to the point, and gorgeously human, flowed from him without let or hindrance. That masterpiece of corresponding, "The German March Through Brussels," was probably written almost as fast as he could talk (next to Phillips Brooks, he was the fastest t□alker I ever heard), but when it came to fiction he had no facility at all. Perhaps I should say that he held in contempt any facility that he may have had. It was owing to his incomparable energy and Joblike patience that he ever gave us any fiction at all. Every phrase in his fiction was, of all the myriad phrases he could think of, the fittest in his relentless judgment to survive. Phrases, paragraphs, pages, whole stories even, were written over and over again. He worked upon a principle of elimination. If he wished to describe an automobile turning in at a gate, he made first a long and elaborate description from which there was omitted no detail, which the most observant pair of eyes in Christendom had ever noted with reference to just such a turning. Thereupon he would begin a process of omitting one by one those details which he had been at such pains to recall; and after each omission he would ask himself: "Does the picture remain?" If it did not, he restored the detail which he had just omitted, and experimented with the sacrifice of some other, and so on, and so on, until after Herculean labor there remained for the reader one of those swiftly flashed, ice-clear pictures (complete in every detail) with which his tales and romances are so delightfully and continuously adorned.

But it is quarter to eleven, and, this being a time of holiday, R. H. D. emerges from his workroom happy to think that he has placed one hundred and seven words between himself and the wolf who hangs about every writer's door. He isn't satisfied with those hundred and seven words. He never was in the least satisfied with anything that he wrote, but he has searched his mind and his conscience and he believes that under the circumstances they are the very best that he can do. Anyway, they can stand in their present order until - after lunch.

A sign of his youth was the fact that to the day of his death he had denied himself the luxury and slothfulness of habits. I have never seen him smoke automatically as most men do. He had too much respect for his own powers of enjoyment and for the sensibilities, perhaps, of the best Havana tobacco. At a time of his own deliberate choosing, often after many hours of hankering and renunciation, he smoked his cigar. He smoked it with delight, with a sense of being rewarded, and he used all the smoke there was in it.

He dearly loved the best food, the best champagne, and the best Scotch whiskey. But these things were friends to him, and not enemies. He had toward food and drink the Continental attitude; namely, that quality is far more important than quantity; and he got his exhilaration from the fact that he was drinking champagne and not from the champagne. Perhaps I shall do well to say that on questions of right and wrong he had a will of iron. All his life he moved resolutely in whichever direction his conscience pointed; and, although that ever present and never obtrusive conscience of his made mistakes of judgment now and then, as must all consciences, I think it can never once have tricked him into any action that was impure or unclean. Some critics maintain that the heroes and heroines of his books are impossibly pure and innocent young people. R. H. D. never called upon his characters for any trait of virtue, or renunciation, or self-mastery of which his own life could not furnish examples.

Fortunately, he did not have for his friends the same conscience that he had for himself. His great gift of eyesight and observation failed him in his judgments upon his friends. If only you loved him, you could get your biggest failures of conduct somewhat more than forgiven, without any trouble at all. And of your mole-hill virtues he made splendid mountains. He only interfered with you when he was afraid that you were going to hurt some one else whom he also loved. Once I had a telegram from him which urged me for heaven's sake not to forget that the next day was my wife's birthday. Whether I had forgotten it or not is my own private affair. And when I declared that I had read a story which I liked very, very much and was going to write to the author to tell him so, he always kept at me till the letter was written.

Have I said that he had no habits? Every day, when he was away from her, he wrote a letter to his mother, and no swift scrawl at that, for, no matter how crowded and eventful the day, he wrote her the best letter that he could write. That was the only habit he had. He was a slave to it.

Once I saw R. H. D. greet his old mother after an absence. They threw their arms about each other and rocked to and fro for a long time. And it hadn't been a long absence at that. No ocean had been between them; her heart had not been in her mouth with the thought that he was under fire, or about to become a victim of jungle fever. He had only been away upon a little expedition, a mere matter of digging for buried treasure. We had found the treasure, part of it a chipmunk's skull and a broken arrow-head, and R. H. D. had been absent from his mother for nearly two hours and a half.

I set about this article with the knowledge that I must fail to give more than a few hints of what he was like. There isn't much more space at my command, and there were so many sides to him that to touch upon them all would fill a volume. There were the patriotism and the Americanism, as much a part of him as the marrow of his bones, and from which sprang all those brilliant headlong letters to the newspapers; those trenchant assaults upon evil-doers in public office, those quixotic efforts to redress wrongs, and those simple and dexterous exposures of this and that, from an absolutely unexpected point of view. He was a quickener of the public conscience. That people are beginning to think tolerantly of preparedness, that a nation which at one time looked yellow as a dandelion is beginning to turn Red, White, and Blue is owing in some measure to him.

R. H. D. thought that war was unspeakably terrible. He thought that peace at the price which our country has been forced to pay for it was infinitely worse. And he was one of those who have gradually taught this country to see the matter in the same way.

I must come to a close now, and I have hardly scratched the surface of my subject. And that is a failure which I feel keenly but which was inevitable. As R. H. D. himself used to say of those deplorable "personal interviews" which appear in the newspapers, and in which the important person interviewed is made by the cub reporter to say things which he never said, or thought, or dreamed of - "You can't expect a fifteen-dollar-a-week brain to describe a thousand-dollar-a-week brain."

There is , however , one question which I should attempt to answer. No two men are alike. In what one salient thing did R. H. D. differ from other men - differ in his personal character and in the character of his work? And that question I can answer offhand, without taking thought, and be sure that I am right.

An analysis of his works, a study of that book which the Recording Angel keeps will show one dominant characteristic to which even his brilliancy, his clarity of style, his excellent mechanism as a writer are subordinate; and to which, as a man, even his sense of duty, his powers of affection, of forgiveness, of loving-kindness are subordinate, too; and that characteristic is cleanliness.

The biggest force for cleanliness that was in the world has gone out of the world - gone to that Happy Hunting Ground where "Nobody hunts us and there is nothing to hunt."

GOUVERNEUR MORRIS.

Chapter 1

THE RED CROSS GIRL

When Spencer Flagg laid the foundation-stone for the new million-dollar wing he was adding to the Flagg Home for Convalescents, on the hills above Greenwich, the New York REPUBLIC sent Sam Ward to cover the story, and with him Redding to take photographs. It was a crisp, beautiful day in October, full of sunshine and the joy of living, and from the great lawn in front of the Home you could see half over Connecticut and across the waters of the Sound to Oyster Bay.

Upon Sam Ward, however, the beauties of Nature were wasted. When, the night previous, he had been given the assignment he had sulked, and he was still sulking. Only a year before he had graduated into New York from a small up-state college and a small up-state newspaper, but already he was a "star" man, and Hewitt, the city editor, humored him.

"What's the matter with the story?" asked the city editor. "With the speeches and lists of names it ought to run to two columns."

"Suppose it does!" exclaimed Ward; "anybody can collect type-written speeches and lists of names. That's a messenger boy's job. Where's there any heart-interest in a Wall Street broker like Flagg waving a silver trowel and singing, 'See what a good boy am!' and a lot of grownup men in pinafores saying, 'This stone is well and truly laid.' Where's the story in that?"

"When I was a reporter," declared the city editor, "I used to be glad to get a day in the country."

"Because you'd never lived in the country," returned Sam. "If you'd wasted twenty-six years in the backwoods, as I did, you'd know that every minute you spend outside of New York you're robbing yourself."

"Of what?" demanded the city editor. "There's nothing to New York except cement, iron girders, noise, and zinc garbage cans. You never see the sun in New York; you never see the moon unless you stand in the middle of the street and bend backward. We never see flowers in New York except on the women's hats. We never see the women except in cages in the elevators - they spend their lives shooting up and down elevator shafts in department stores, in apartment houses, in office buildings. And we never see children in New York because the janitors won't let the women who live in elevators have children! Don't talk to me! New York's a Little Nemo nightmare. It's a joke. It's an insult!"

"How curious!" said Sam. "Now I see why they took you off the street and made you a city editor. I don't agree with anything you say. Especially are you wrong about the women. They ought to be caged in elevators, but they're not. Instead, they flash past you in the street; they shine upon you from boxes in the theatre; they frown at you from the tops of buses; they smile at you from the cushions of a taxi, across restaurant tables under red candle shades, when you offer them a seat in the subway. They are the only thing in New York that gives me any trouble."

The city editor sighed. "How young you are!" he exclaimed. "However, to-morrow you will be free from your only trouble. There will be few women at the celebration, and they will be interested only in convalescents - and you do not look like a convalescent."

Sam Ward sat at the outer edge of the crowd of overdressed females and overfed men, and, with a sardonic smile, listened to Flagg telling his assembled friends and sycophants how glad he was they were there to see him give away a million dollars.

"Aren't you going to get his speech?", asked Redding, the staff photographer.

"Get HIS speech!" said Sam. "They have Pinkertons all over the grounds to see that you don't escape with less than three copies. I'm waiting to hear the ritual they always have, and then I'm going to sprint for the first train back to the centre of civilization."

"There's going to be a fine lunch," said Redding, "and reporters are expected. I asked the policeman if we were, and he said we were."

Sam rose, shook his trousers into place, stuck his stick under his armpit and smoothed his yellow gloves. He was very thoughtful of his clothes and always treated them with courtesy.

"You can have my share," he said. "I cannot forget that

I am fifty-five minutes from Broadway. And even if I were starving I would rather have a club sandwich in New York than a Thanksgiving turkey dinner in New Rochelle."

He nodded and with eager, athletic strides started toward the iron gates; but he did not reach the iron gates, for on the instant trouble barred his way. Trouble came to him wearing the blue cambric uniform of a nursing sister, with a red cross on her arm, with a white collar turned down, white cuffs turned back, and a tiny black velvet bonnet. A bow of white lawn chucked her impudently under the chin. She had hair like golden-rod and eyes as blue as flax, and a complexion of such health and cleanliness and dewiness as blooms only on trained nurses.

She was so lovely that Redding swung his hooded camera at her as swiftly as a cowboy could have covered her with his gun.

Reporters become star reporters because they observe things that other people miss and because they do not let it appear that they have observed them. When the great man who is being interviewed blurts out that which is indiscreet but most important, the cub reporter says: "That's most interesting, sir. I'll make a note of that." And so warns the great man into silence. But the star reporter receives the indiscreet utterance as though it bored him; and the great man does not know he has blundered until he reads of it the next morning under screaming headlines.

Other men, on being suddenly confronted by Sister Anne, which was the official title of the nursing sister, would have fallen backward, or swooned, or gazed at her with soulful, worshipping eyes; or, were they that sort of beast, would have ogled her with impertinent approval. Now Sam, because he was a star reporter, observed that the lady before him was the most beautiful young woman he had ever seen; but no one would have guessed that he observed that - least of all Sister Anne. He stood in her way and lifted his hat, and even looked into the eyes of blue as impersonally and as calmly as though she were his great-aunt - as though his heart was not beating so fast that it choked him.

"I am from the REPUBLIC," he said. "Everybody is so busy here to-day that I'm not able to get what I need about the Home. It seems a pity," he added disappointedly, "because it's so well done that people ought to know about it." He frowned at the big hospital buildings. It was apparent that the ignorance of the public concerning their excellence greatly annoyed him.

When again he looked at Sister Anne she was regarding him in alarm - obviously she was upon the point of instant flight.

"You are a reporter?" she said.

Some people like to place themselves in the hands of a reporter because they hope he will print their names in black letters; a few others - only reporters know how few - would as soon place themselves in the hands of a dentist.

"A reporter from the REPUBLIC," repeated Sam.

"But why ask ME?" demanded Sister Anne.

Sam could see no reason for her question; in extenuation and explanation he glanced at her uniform.

"I thought you were at work here," he said simply. "I beg your pardon."

He stepped aside as though he meant to leave her. In giving that impression he was distinctly dishonest.

"There was no other reason," persisted Sister Anne. "I mean for speaking to me?"

The reason for speaking to her was so obvious that Sam wondered whether this could be the height of innocence or the most banal coquetry. The hostile look in the eyes of the lady proved it could not be coquetry.

"I am sorry," said Sam. "I mistook you for one of the nurses here; and, as you didn't seem busy, I thought you might give me some statistics about the Home not really statistics, you know, but local color."

Sister Anne returned his look with one as steady as his own. Apparently she was weighing his statement. She seemed to disbelieve it. Inwardly he was asking himself what could be the dark secret in the past of this young woman that at the mere approach of a reporter - even of such a nice-looking reporter as himself - she should shake and shudder. "If that's what you really want to know," said Sister Anne doubtfully," I'll try and help you; but," she added, looking at him as one who issues an ultimatum, "you must not say anything about me!"

Sam knew that a woman of the self-advertising, club-organizing class will always say that to a reporter at the time she gives him her card so that he can spell her name correctly; but Sam recognized that this young woman meant it. Besides, what was there that he could write about her? Much as he might like to do so, he could not begin his story with: "The Flagg Home for Convalescents is also the home of the most beautiful of all living women." No copy editor would let that get by him. So, as there was nothing to say that he would be allowed to say, he promised to say nothing. Sister Anne smiled; and it seemed to Sam that she smiled, not because his promise had set her mind at ease, but because the promise amused her. Sam wondered why.

Sister Anne fell into step beside him and led him through the wards of the hospital. He found that it existed for and revolved entirely about one person. He found that a million dollars and some acres of buildings, containing sun-rooms and hundreds of rigid white beds, had been donated by Spencer Flagg only to provide a background for Sister Anne - only to exhibit the depth of her charity, the kindness of her heart, the unselfishness of her nature.

"Do you really scrub the floors?" he demanded - "I mean you yourself - down on your knees, with a pail and water and scrubbing brush?"

Sister Anne raised her beautiful eyebrows and laughed at him.

"We do that when we first come here," she said - "when we are probationers. Is there a newer way of scrubbing floors?"

"And these awful patients," demanded Sam - "do you wait on them? Do you have to submit to their complaints and whinings and ingratitude?" He glared at the unhappy convalescents as though by that glance he would annihilate them. "It's not fair!" exclaimed Sam. "It's ridiculous. I'd like to choke them!"

"That's not exactly the object of a home for convalescents," said Sister Anne.

"You know perfectly well what I mean," said Sam. "Here are you - if you'll allow me to say so - a magnificent, splendid, healthy young person, wearing out your young life over a lot of lame ducks, failures, and cripples."

"Nor is that quite the way we look at," said Sister Anne.

"We?" demanded Sam.

Sister Anne nodded toward a group of nurse

"I'm not the only nurse here," she said "There are over forty."

"You are the only one here," said Sam, "who is not! That's Just what I mean - I appreciate the work of a trained nurse; I understand the ministering angel part of it; but you - I'm not talking about anybody else; I'm talking about you - you are too young! Somehow you are different; you are not meant to wear yourself out fighting disease and sickness, measuring beef broth and making beds."

Sister Anne laughed with delight.

"I beg your pardon," said Sam stiffly.

"No - pardon me," said Sister Anne; "but your ideas of the duties of a nurse are so quaint."

"No matter what the duties are," declared Sam; "You should not be here!"

Sister Anne shrugged her shoulders; they were charming shoulders - as delicate as the pinions of a bird.

"One must live," said Sister Anne.

They had passed through the last cold corridor, between the last rows of rigid white cots, and had come out into the sunshine. Below them stretched Connecticut, painted in autumn colors. Sister Anne seated herself upon the marble railing of the terrace and looked down upon the flashing waters of the Sound.

"Yes; that's it," she repeated softly - "one must live."

Sam looked at her - but, finding that to do so made speech difficult, looked hurriedly away. He admitted to himself that it was one of those occasions, only too frequent with him, when his indignant sympathy was heightened by the fact that "the woman. was very fair." He conceded that. He was not going to pretend to himself that he was not prejudiced by the outrageous beauty of Sister Anne, by the assault upon his feelings made by her uniform - made by the appeal of her profession, the gentlest and most gracious of all professions. He was honestly disturbed that this young girl should devote her life to the service of selfish sick people.

"If you do it because you must live, then it can easily be arranged; for there are other ways of earning a living."

The girl looked at him quickly, but he was quite sincere - and again she smiled.

"Now what would you suggest?" she asked. "You see," she said, "I have no one to advise me - no man of my own age. I have no brothers to go to. I have a father, but it was his idea that I should come here; and so I doubt if he would approve of my changing to any other work. Your own work must make you acquainted with many women who earn their own living. Maybe you could advise me?"

Sam did not at once answer. He was calculating hastily how far his salary would go toward supporting a wife. He was trying to remember which of the men in the office were married, and whether they were those whose salaries were smaller than his own. Collins, one of the copy editors, he knew, was very ill-paid; but Sam also knew that Collins was married, because his wife used to wait for him in the office to take her to the theatre, and often Sam had thought she was extremely well dressed. Of course Sister Anne was so beautiful that what she might wear would be a matter of indifference; but then women did not always look at it that way. Sam was so long considering offering Sister Anne a life position that his silence had become significant; and to cover his real thoughts he said hurriedly:

"Take type-writing, for instance. That pays very well. The hours are not difficult."

"And manicuring?" suggested Sister Anne.

Sam exclaimed in horror.

"You!" he cried roughly. "For you! Quite impossible!"

"Why for me?" said the girl.

In the distress at the thought Sam was jabbing his stick into the gravel walk as though driving the manicuring idea into a deep grave. He did not see that the girl was smiling at him mockingly.

"You?" protested Sam. "You in a barber's shop washing men's fingers who are not fit to wash the streets you walk on I Good Lord!" His vehemence was quite honest. The girl ceased smiling. Sam was still jabbing at the gravel walk, his profile toward her - and, unobserved, she could study his face. It was an attractive face strong, clever, almost illegally good-looking. It explained why, as , he had complained to the city editor, his chief trouble in New York was with the women. With his eyes full of concern, Sam turned to her abruptly. "How much do they give you a month?" "Forty dollars," answered Sister Anne. "This is what hurts me about it," said Sam.

It is that you should have to work and wait on other people when there are so many strong, hulking men who would count it God's blessing to work for you, to wait on you, and give their lives for you. However, probably you know that better than I do."

"No; I don't know that," said Sister Anne.

Sam recognized that it was quite absurd that it should

be so, but this statement gave him a sense of great elation, a delightful thrill of relief. There was every reason why the girl should not confide in a complete stranger - even to deceive him was quite within her rights; but, though Sam appreciated this, he preferred to be deceived.

"I think you are working too hard," he said, smiling happily. "I think you ought to have a change. You ought to take a day off! Do they ever give you a day off?"

"Next Saturday," said Sister Anne. "Why?"

"Because," explained Sam, "if you won't think it too presumptuous, I was going to prescribe a day off for you - a day entirely away from iodoform and white enamelled cots. It is what you need, a day in the city and a lunch where they have music; and a matinee, where you can laugh - or cry, if you like that better - and then, maybe, some fresh air in the park in a taxi; and after that dinner and more theatre, and then I'll see you safe on the train for Greenwich. Before you answer," he added hurriedly, "I want to explain that I contemplate taking a day off myself and doing all these things with you, and that if you want to bring any of the other forty nurses along as a chaperon, I hope you will. Only, honestly, I hope you won't!"

The proposal apparently gave Sister Anne much pleasure. She did not say so, but her eyes shone and when she looked at Sam she was almost laughing with happiness.

"I think that would be quite delightful," said Sister Anne," - quite delightful! Only it would be frightfully expensive; even if I don't bring another girl, which I certainly would not, it would cost a great deal of money. I think we might cut out the taxicab - and walk in the park and feed the squirrels."

"Oh!" exclaimed Sam in disappointment, - "then you know Central Park?"

Sister Anne's eyes grew quite expressionless.

"I once lived near there," she said.

"In Harlem?"

"Not exactly in Harlem, but near it. I was quite young," said Sister Anne. "Since then I have always lived in the country or in - other places."

Sam's heart was singing with pleasure.

"It's so kind of you to consent," he cried. "Indeed, you are the kindest person in all the world. I thought so when I saw you bending over these sick people, and, now I know."

"It is you who are kind," protested Sister Anne, "to take pity on me."

"Pity on you!" laughed Sam. "You can't pity a person who can do more with a smile than old man Flagg can do with all his millions. Now," he demanded in happy anticipation," where are we to meet?"

"That's it," said Sister Anne. "Where are we to meet?"

" Let it be at the Grand Central Station. The day can't

begin too soon," said Sam; "and before then telephone me what theatre and restaurants you want and I'll reserve seats and tables. Oh," exclaimed Sam joyfully, "it will be a wonderful day - a wonderful day!"

Sister Anne looked at him curiously and, so, it seemed, a little wistfully. She held out her hand.

"I must go back to my duties," she said. "Good-by."

" Not good-by , " said Sam heartily, "only until Saturday - and my name's Sam Ward and my address is the city room of the REPUBLIC. What's your name?"

"Sister Anne," said the girl. "In the nursing order to which I belong we have no last names."

"So," asked Sam, "I'll call you Sister Anne?"

"No; just Sister," said the girl.

"Sister!" repeated Sam, "Sister!" He breathed the word rather than spoke it; and the way he said it and the way he looked when he said it made it carry almost the touch of a caress. It was as if he had said "Sweetheart! or "Beloved!" "I'll not forget," said Sam.

Sister Anne gave an impatient, annoyed laugh.

"Nor I," she said.

Sam returned to New York in the smoking-car, puffing feverishly at his cigar and glaring dreamily at the smoke. He was living the day over again and, in anticipation, the day off, still to come. He rehearsed their next meeting at the station; he considered whether or not he would meet her with a huge bunch of violets or would have it brought to her when they were at luncheon by the head waiter. He decided the latter way would be more of a pleasant surprise. He planned the luncheon. It was to be the most marvellous repast he could evolve; and, lest there should be the slightest error, he would have it prepared in advance - and it should cost half his week's salary.

The place where they were to dine he would leave to her, because he had observed that women had strange ideas about clothes - some of them thinking that certain clothes must go with certain restaurants. Some of them seemed to believe that, instead of their conferring distinction upon the restaurant, the restaurant conferred distinction upon them. He was sure Sister Anne would not be so foolish, but it might be that she must always wear her nurse's uniform and that she would prefer not to be conspicuous; so he decided that the choice of where they would dine he would leave to her. He calculated that the whole day ought to cost about eighty dollars, which, as star reporter, was what he was then earning each week. That was little enough to give for a day that would be the birthday of his life! No, he contradicted - the day he had first met her must always be the birthday of his life; for never had he met one like her and he was sure there never would be one like her. She was so entirely superior to all the others, so fine, so difficult - in her manner there was something that rendered her unapproachable. Even her simple nurse's gown was worn with a difference. She might have been a princess in fancy dress. And yet, how humble she had been when he begged her to let him for one day personally conduct her over the great city! "You are so kind to take pity on me," she had said. He thought of many clever, pretty speeches he might have made. He was so annoyed he had not thought of them at the time that he kicked violently at the seat in front of him.

He wondered what her history might be; he was sure it was full of beautiful courage and self-sacrifice. It certainly was outrageous that one so glorious must work for her living, and for such a paltry living - forty dollars a month! It was worth that merely to have her sit in the flat where one could look at her; for already he had decided that, when they were married, they would live in a flat - probably in one overlooking Central Park, on Central Park West. He knew of several attractive suites there at thirty-five dollars a week - or, if she preferred the suburbs, he would forsake his beloved New York and return to the country. In his gratitude to her for being what she was, he conceded even that sacrifice.

When he reached New York, from the speculators he bought front-row seats at five dollars for the two most popular plays in town. He put them away carefully in his waistcoat pocket. Possession of them made him feel that already he had obtained an option on six hours of complete happiness.

After she left Sam, Sister Anne passed hurriedly through the hospital to the matron's room and, wrapping herself in a raccoon coat, made her way to a waiting motor car and said, "Home!" to the chauffeur. He drove her to the Flagg family vault, as Flagg's envious millionaire neighbors called the pile of white marble that topped the highest hill above Greenwich, and which for years had served as a landfall to mariners on the Sound.

There were a number of people at tea when she arrived and they greeted her noisily.

"I have had a most splendid adventure!" said Sister Anne. "There were six of us, you know, dressed up as Red Cross nurses, and we gave away programmes. Well, one of the New York reporters thought I was a real nurse and interviewed me about the Home. Of course I knew enough about it to keep it up, and I kept it up so well that he was terribly sorry for me; and. . ."

One of the tea drinkers was little Hollis Holworthy, who prided himself on knowing who's who in New York. He had met Sam Ward at first nights and prize fights. He laughed scornfully.

"Don't you believe it!" he interrupted. "That man who was talking to you was Sam Ward. He's the smartest newspaper man in New York; he was just leading you on. Do you suppose there's a reporter in America who wouldn't know you in the dark? Wait until you see the Sunday paper."

Sister Anne exclaimed indignantly.

"He did not know me!" she protested. "It quite upset him that I should be wasting my life measuring out medicines and making beds."

There was a shriek of disbelief and laughter.

"I told him," continued Sister Anne, "that I got forty dollars a month, and he said I could make more as a typewriter; and I said I preferred to be a manicurist."

"Oh, Anita!" protested the admiring chorus.

"And he was most indignant. He absolutely refused to allow me to be a manicurist. And he asked me to take a day off with him and let him show me New York. And he offered, as attractions, moving-picture shows and a drive on a Fifth Avenue bus, and feeding peanuts to the animals in the park. And if I insisted upon a chaperon I might bring one of the nurses. We're to meet at the soda-water fountain in the Grand Central Station. He said, 'The day cannot begin too soon.'"

"Oh, Anita!" shrieked the chorus.

Lord Deptford, who as the newspapers had repeatedly informed the American public, had come to the Flaggs' country-place to try to marry Anita Flagg, was amused.

"What an awfully jolly rag!" he cried. "And what are you going to do about it?"

"Nothing," said Anita Flagg. "The reporters have been making me ridiculous for the last three years; now I have got back at one of them! "And," she added, "that's all there is to that!"

That night, however, when the house party was making toward bed, Sister Anne stopped by the stairs and said to Lord Deptford: "I want to hear you call me Sister."

"Call you what?" exclaimed the young man. "I will tell you," he whispered, "what I'd like to call you!"

"You will not!" interrupted Anita. "Do as I tell you and say Sister once. Say it as though you meant it."

"But I don't mean it," protested his lordship. "I've said already what I. . . ."

"Never mind what you've said already," commanded Miss Flagg. "I've heard that from a lot of people. Say Sister just once."

His lordship frowned in embarrassment.

"Sister!" he exclaimed. It sounded like the pop of a cork.

Anita Flagg laughed unkindly and her beautiful shoulders shivered as though she were cold.

"Not a bit like it, Deptford," she said. "Good-night."

Later Helen Page, who came to her room to ask her about a horse she was to ride in the morning, found her ready for bed but standing by the open window looking out toward the great city to the south.

When she turned Miss Page saw something in her eyes that caused that young woman to shriek with amazement.

"Anita!" she exclaimed. "You crying! What in Heaven's name can make you cry?"

It was not a kind speech, nor did Miss Flagg receive it kindly. She turned upon the tactless intruder.

"Suppose," cried Anita fiercely, "a man thought you were worth forty dollars a month - honestly didn't know! - honestly believed you were poor and worked for your living, and still said your smile was worth more than all of old man Flagg's millions, not knowing they were YOUR millions. Suppose he didn't ask any money of you, but just to take care of you, to slave for you - only wanted to keep your pretty hands from working, and your pretty eyes from seeing sickness and pain. Suppose you met that man among this rotten lot, what would you do? What wouldn't you do?"

"Why, Anita!" exclaimed Miss Page.

"What would you do?" demanded Anita Flagg. "This is what you'd do: You'd go down on your knees to that man and say: 'Take me away! Take me away from them, and pity me, and be sorry for me, and love me - and love me - and love me!"

"And why don't you?" cried Helen Page.

"Because I'm as rotten as the rest of them!" cried Anita Flagg. "Because I'm a coward. And that's why I'm crying. Haven't I the right to cry?"

At the exact moment Miss Flagg was proclaiming herself a moral coward, in the local room of the REPUBLIC Collins, the copy editor, was editing Sam's story' of the laying of the corner-stone. The copy editor's cigar was tilted near his left eyebrow; his blue pencil, like a guillotine ready to fall upon the guilty word or paragraph, was suspended in mid-air; and continually, like a hawk preparing to strike, the blue pencil swooped and circled. But page after page fell softly to the desk and the blue pencil remained inactive. As he read, the voice of Collins rose in muttered ejaculations; and, as he continued to read, these explosions grew louder and more amazed. At last he could endure no more and, swinging swiftly in his revolving chair, his glance swept the office. "In the name of Mike!" he shouted. "What IS this?"

The reporters nearest him, busy with pencil and typewriters, frowned in impatient protest. Sam Ward, swinging his legs from the top of a table, was gazing at the ceiling, wrapped in dreams and tobacco smoke. Upon his clever, clean-cut features the expression was far-away and beatific. He came back to earth.

"What's what?" Sam demanded.

At that moment Elliott, the managing editor, was passing through the room his hands filled with freshly pulled proofs. He swung toward Collins quickly and snatched up Sam's copy. The story already was late - and it was important.

"What's wrong?" he demanded. Over the room there fell a sudden hush.

"Read the opening paragraph," protested Collins. "It's like that for a column! It's all about a girl - about a Red Cross nurse. Not a word about Flagg or Lord Deptford. No speeches! No news! It's not a news story at all. It's an editorial, and an essay, and a spring poem. I don't know what it is. And, what's worse," wailed the copy editor defiantly and to the amazement of all, "it's so darned good that you can't touch it. You've got to let it go or kill it."

The eyes of the managing editor, masked by his green paper shade, were racing over Sam's written words. He thrust the first page back at Collins.

"Is it all like that?"

"There's a column like that!"

"Run it just as it is," commanded the managing editor. " Use it for your introduction and get your story from the flimsy. And, in your head, cut out Flagg entirely. Call it 'The Red Cross Girl.' And play it up strong with pictures." He turned on Sam and eyed him curiously.

" What's the idea , Ward ? " he said. " This is a newspaper - not a magazine!"

The click of the typewriters was silent, the hectic rush of the pencils had ceased, and the staff, expectant, smiled cynically upon the star reporter. Sam shoved his hands into his trousers pockets and also smiled, but unhappily.

"I know it's not news, Sir," he said; but that's the way I saw the story - outside on the lawn, the band playing, and the governor and the governor's staff and the clergy burning incense to Flagg; and inside, this girl right on the job - taking care of the sick and wounded. It seemed to me that a million from a man that won't miss a million didn't stack up against what this girl was doing for these sick folks! What I wanted to say," continued Sam stoutly "was that the moving spirit of the hospital was not in the man who signed the checks, but in these women who do the work - the nurses, like the one I wrote about; the one you called 'The Red Cross Girl.'"

Collins, strong through many years of faithful service, backed by the traditions of the profession, snorted scornfully.

"But it's not news!"

"It's not news," said Elliott doubtfully; "but it's the kind of story that made Frank O'Malley famous. It's the kind of story that drives men out of this business into the arms of what Kipling calls 'the illegitimate sister.'"

It seldom is granted to a man on the same day to give his whole heart to a girl and to be patted on the back by his managing editor; and it was this combination, and not the drinks he dispensed to the staff in return for its congratulations, that sent Sam home walking on air. He loved his business, he was proud of his business; but never before had it served him so well. It had enabled him to tell the woman he loved, and incidentally a million other people, how deeply he honored her; how clearly he appreciated her power for good. No one would know he meant Sister Anne, save two people - Sister Anne and himself; but for her and for him that was as many as should know. In his story he had used real incidents of the day; he had described her as she passed through the wards of the hospital, cheering and sympathetic; he had told of the little acts of consideration that endeared her to the sick people.

The next morning she would know that it was she of whom he had written; and between the lines she would read that the man who wrote them loved her. So he fell asleep, impatient for the morning. In the hotel at which he lived the REPUBLIC was always placed promptly outside his door; and, after many excursions into the hall, he at last found it. On the front page was his story, "The Red Cross Girl." It had the place of honor - right-hand column; but more conspicuous than the headlines of his own story was one of Redding's, photographs. It was the one he had taken of Sister Anne when first she had approached them, in her uniform of mercy, advancing across the lawn, walking straight into the focus of the, camera. There was no mistaking her for any other living woman; but beneath the picture, in bold, staring, uncompromising type, was a strange and grotesque legend.

"Daughter of Millionaire Flagg," it read, "in a New Role, Miss Anita Flagg as The Red Cross Girl."

For a long time Sam looked at the picture, and then, folding the paper so that the picture was hidden, he walked to the open window. From below, Broadway sent up a tumultuous greeting - cable cars jangled, taxis hooted; and, on the sidewalks, on their way to work, processions of shop-girls stepped out briskly. It was the street and the city and the life he had found fascinating, but now it jarred and affronted him. A girl he knew had died, had passed out of his life forever - worse than that had never existed; and yet the city went or just as though that made no difference, or just as little difference as it would have made had Sister Anne really lived and really died.

At the same early hour, an hour far too early for the rest of the house party, Anita Flagg and Helen Page, booted and riding-habited, sat alone at the breakfast table, their tea before them; and in the hands of Anita Flagg was the DAILY REPUBLIC. Miss Page had brought the paper to the table and, with affected indignation at the impertinence of the press, had pointed at the front-page photograph; but Miss Flagg was not looking at the photograph, or drinking her tea, or showing in her immediate surroundings any interest whatsoever. Instead, her lovely eyes were fastened with fascination upon the column under the heading "The Red Cross Girl"; and, as she read, the lovely eyes lost all trace of recent slumber, her lovely lips parted breathlessly, and on her lovely cheeks the color flowed and faded and glowed and bloomed. When she had read as far as a paragraph beginning, "When Sister Anne walked between them those who suffered raised their eyes to hers as flowers lift their faces to the rain," she dropped the paper and started for telephone.

"Any man," cried she, to the mutual discomfort of Helen Page and the servants, "who thinks I'm like that mustn't get away! I'm not like that and I know it; but if he thinks so that's all I want. And maybe I might be like that - if any man would help."

She gave her attention to the telephone and "Information." She demanded to be instantly put into communication with the DAILY REPUBLIC and Mr. Sam Ward. She turned again upon Helen Page.

"I'm tired of being called a good sport," she protested, "by men who aren't half so good sports as I am. I'm tired of being talked to about money - as though I were a stock-broker. This man's got a head on his shoulders, and he's got the shoulders too; and he's got a darned good-looking head; and he thinks I'm a ministering angel and a saint; and he put me up on a pedestal and made me dizzy - and I like being made dizzy; and I'm for him! And I'm going after him!"

"Be still!" implored Helen Page. "Any one might think you meant it!" She nodded violently at the discreet backs of the men-servants.

"Ye gods, Parker!" cried Anita Flagg. "Does it take three of you to pour a cup of tea? Get out of here, and tell everybody that you all three caught me in the act of proposing to an American gentleman over the telephone and that the betting is even that I'll make him marry me!"

The faithful and sorely tried domestics fled toward the door. "And what's more," Anita hurled after them, "get your bets down quick, for after I meet him the odds will be a hundred to one!"

Had the REPUBLIC been an afternoon paper, Sam might have been at the office and might have gone to the telephone, and things might have happened differently; but, as the REPUBLIC was a morning paper, the only person in the office was the lady who scrubbed the floors and she refused to go near the telephone. So Anita Flagg said, "I'll call him up later," and went happily on her ride, with her heart warm with love for all the beautiful world; but later it was too late.

To keep himself fit, Sam Ward always walked to the office. On this particular morning Hollis Holworthy was walking uptown and they met opposite the cathedral.

"You're the very man I want," said Hollworthy joyously - "you've got to decide a bet."

He turned and fell into step with Sam.

"It's one I made last night with Anita Flagg. She thinks you didn't know who she was yesterday, and I said that was ridiculous. Of course you knew. I bet her a theatre party."

To Sam it seemed hardly fair that so soon, before his fresh wound had even been dressed, it should be torn open by impertinent fingers; but he had no right to take offense. How could the man, or any one else, know what Sister Anne had meant to him?

"I'm afraid you lose," he said. He halted to give Holworthy the hint to leave him, but Holworthy had no such intention.

"You don't say so!" exclaimed that young man. "Fancy one of you chaps being taken in like that. "I thought you were taking her in - getting up a story for the Sunday supplement."

Sam shook his head, nodded, and again moved on; but he was not yet to escape. "And, instead of your fooling her," exclaimed Holworthy incredulously, "she was having fun, with you!"

With difficulty Sam smiled.

"So it would seem," he said.

"She certainly made an awfully funny story of it!" exclaimed Holworthy admiringly. "I thought she was making it up - she must have made some of it up. She said you asked her to take a day off in New York. That isn't so is it?"

"Yes, that's so."

"By Jove!" cried Holworthy - and that you invited her to see the moving-picture shows?"

Sam, conscious of the dearly bought front row seats in his pocket, smiled pleasantly.

"Did she say I said that - or you?" he asked

"She did."

"Well, then, I must have said it."

Holworthy roared with amusement.

"And that you invited her to feed peanuts to the monkeys at the Zoo?"

Sam avoided the little man's prying eyes.

"Yes; I said that too."

"And I thought she was making it up!" exclaimed Holworthy. "We did laugh. You must see the fun of it yourself."

Lest Sam should fail to do so he proceeded to elaborate.

"You must see the fun in a man trying to make a date with Anita Flagg - just as if she were nobody!"

"I don't think," said Sam, "that was my idea." He waved his stick at a passing taxi. "I'm late," he said. He abandoned Hollis on the sidewalk, chuckling and grinning with delight, and unconscious of the mischief he had made.

An hour later at the office, when Sam was waiting for an assignment, the telephone boy hurried to him, his eyes lit with excitement.

"You're wanted on the 'phone," he commanded. His voice dropped to an awed whisper. "Miss Anita Flagg wants to speak to you!"

The blood ran leaping to Sam's heart and face. Then he remembered that this was not Sister Anne who wanted to speak to him, but a woman he had never met.

"Say you can't find me," he directed. The boy gasped, fled, and returned precipitately.

"The lady says she wants your telephone number - says she must have it."

"Tell her you don't know it; tell her it's against the rules - and hang up."

Ten minutes later the telephone boy, in the strictest confidence, had informed every member of the local staff that Anita Flagg - the rich, the beautiful, the daring, the original of the Red Cross story of that morning - had twice called up Sam Ward and by that young man had been thrown down - and thrown hard!

That night Elliott, the managing editor, sent for Sam; and when Sam entered his office he found also there Walsh, the foreign editor, with whom he was acquainted only by sight.

Elliott introduced them and told Sam to be seated.

"Ward," he began abruptly, "I'm sorry to lose you, but you've got to go. It's on account of that story of this morning."

Sam made no sign, but he was deeply hurt. From a paper he had served so loyally this seemed scurvy treatment. It struck him also that, considering the spirit in which the story had been written, it was causing him more kinds of trouble than was quite fair. The loss of position did not disturb him. In the last month too many managing editors had tried to steal him from the REPUBLIC for him to feel anxious as to the future. So he accepted his dismissal calmly, and could say without resentment:

"Last night I thought you liked the story, sir?

"I did," returned Elliott; "I liked it so much that I'm sending you to a bigger place, where you can get bigger stories. We want you to act as our special correspondent in London. Mr. Walsh will explain the work; and if you'll go you'll sail next Wednesday."

After his talk with the foreign editor Sam again walked home on air. He could not believe it was real - that it was actually to him it had happened; for hereafter he was to witness the march of great events, to come in contact with men of international interests. Instead of reporting what was of concern only from the Battery to Forty-seventh Street, he would now tell New York what was of interest in Europe and the British Empire, and so to the whole world. There was one drawback only to his happiness - there was no one with whom he might divide it. He wanted to celebrate his good fortune; he wanted to share it with some one who would understand how much it meant to him, who would really care. Had Sister Anne lived, she would have understood; and he would have laid himself and his new position at her feet and begged her to accept them - begged her to run away with him to this tremendous and terrifying capital of the world, and start the new life together.

Among all the women he knew, there was none to take her place. Certainly Anita Flagg could not take her place. Not because she was rich, not because she had jeered at him and made him a laughing-stock, not because his admiration - and he blushed when he remembered how openly, how ingenuously he had shown it to her - meant nothing; but because the girl he thought she was, the girl he had made dreams about and wanted to marry without a moment's notice, would have seen that what he offered, ridiculous as it was when offered to Anita Flagg, was not ridiculous when offered sincerely to a tired, nerve-worn, overworked nurse in a hospital. It was because Anita Flagg had not seen that that she could not now make up to him for the girl he had lost, even though she herself had inspired that girl and for a day given her existence.

Had he known it, the Anita Flagg of his imagining was just as unlike and as unfair to the real girl as it was possible for two people to be. His Anita Flagg he had created out of the things he had read of her in impertinent Sunday supplements and from the impression he had been given of her by the little ass, Holworthy. She was not at all like that. Ever since she had come of age she had been beset by sycophants and flatterers, both old and young, both men and girls, and by men who wanted her money and by men who wanted her. And it was because she got the motives of the latter two confused that she was so often hurt and said sharp, bitter things that made her appear hard and heartless.

As a matter of fact, in approaching her in the belief that he was addressing an entirely different person, Sam had got nearer to the real Anita Flagg than had any other man. And so - when on arriving at the office the next morning, which was a Friday, he received a telegram reading, "Arriving to-morrow nine-thirty from Greenwich; the day cannot begin too soon; don't forget you promised to meet me. Anita Flagg " - he was able to reply: " Extremely sorry; but promise made to a different person, who unfortunately has since died!"'

When Anita Flagg read this telegram there leaped to her lovely eyes tears that sprang from self-pity and wounded feelings. She turned miserably, appealingly to Helen Page.

"But why does he do it to me?" Her tone was that of the bewildered child who has struck her head against the table, and from the naughty table, without cause or provocation, has received the devil of a bump.

Before Miss Page could venture upon an explanation, Anita Flagg had changed into a very angry young woman.

"And what's more," she announced, "he can't do it to me!"

She sent her telegram back again as it was, word for word, but this time it was signed, Sister Anne."

In an hour the answer came: "Sister Anne is the person to whom I refer. She is dead."

Sam was not altogether at ease at the outcome of his adventure. It was not in his nature to be rude - certainly not to a woman, especially not to the most beautiful woman he had ever seen. For, whether her name was Anita or Anne, about her beauty there could be no argument; but he assured himself that he had acted within his rights. A girl who could see in a well-meant offer to be kind only a subject for ridicule was of no interest to him. Nor did her telegrams insisting upon continuing their acquaintance flatter him. As he read them, they showed only that she looked upon him as one entirely out of her world - as one with whom she could do an unconventional thing and make a good story about it later, knowing that it would be accepted as one of her amusing caprices.

He was determined he would not lend himself to any such performance. And, besides, he no longer was a foot-loose, happy-go-lucky reporter. He no longer need seek for experiences and material to turn into copy. He was now a man with a responsible position - one who soon would be conferring with cabinet ministers and putting ambassadors At their ease. He wondered if a beautiful heiress, whose hand was sought in marriage by the nobility of England, would understand the importance of a London correspondent. He hoped someone would tell her. He liked to think of her as being considerably impressed and a little unhappy.

Saturday night he went to the theatre for which he had purchased tickets. And he went alone, for the place that Sister Anne was to have occupied could not be filled by any other person. It would have been sacrilege. At least, so it pleased him to pretend. And all through dinner, which he ate alone at the same restaurant to which he had intended taking her, he continued, to pretend she was with him. And at the theatre, where there was going forward the most popular of all musical comedies, the seat next to him, which to the audience, appeared wastefully empty, was to him filled with her gracious presence. That Sister Anne was not there - that the pretty romance he had woven about her had ended in disaster - filled, him with real regret. He was glad he was,, leaving New York. He was glad he was going, where nothing would remind him of her. And then he glanced up - and looked straight into her eyes!

He was seated in the front row, directly on the aisle. The seat Sister Anne was supposed to be occupying was on his right, and a few seats farther to his right rose the stage box and in the stage box, and in the stage box, almost upon the stage, and with the glow of the foot-lights full in her face, was Anita Flagg, smiling delightedly down on him. There were others with her. He had a confused impression of bulging shirt-fronts, and shining silks, and diamonds, and drooping plumes upon enormous hats. He thought he recognized Lord Deptford and Holworthy; but the only person he distinguished clearly was Anita Flagg. The girl was all in black velvet, which was drawn to her figure like a wet bathing suit; round her throat was a single string of pearls, and on her hair of golden-rod was a great hat of black velvet, shaped like a bell, with the curving lips of a lily. And from beneath its brim Anita Flagg, sitting rigidly erect with her white-gloved hands resting lightly on her knee, was gazing down at him, smiling with pleasure, with surprise, with excitement.

When she saw that, in spite of her altered appearance, he recognized her, she bowed so violently and bent her head so eagerly that above her the ostrich plumes dipped and courtesied like wheat in a storm. But Sam neither bowed nor courtesied. Instead, he turned his head slowly over his left shoulder, as though he thought she was speaking not to him but some one beyond him, across the aisle. And then his eyes returned to the stage and did not again look toward her. It was not the cut direct, but it was a cut that hurt; and in their turn the eyes of Miss Flagg quickly sought the stage. At the moment, the people in the audience happened to be laughing; and she forced a smile and then laughed with them.

Out of the corner of his eye Sam could not help seeing her profile exposed pitilessly in the glow of the foot-lights; saw her lips tremble like those of a child about to cry; and then saw the forced, hard smile - and heard her laugh lightly and mechanically.

"That's all she cares." he told himself.

It seemed to him that in all he heard of her, in everything she did, she kept robbing him still further of all that was dear to him in Sister Anne.

For five minutes, conscious of the foot-lights, Miss Flagg maintained upon her lovely face a fixed and intent expression, and then slowly and unobtrusively drew back to a seat in the rear of the box. In the' darkest recesses she found Holworthy, shut off from a view of the stage by a barrier of women's hats.

"Your friend Mr. Ward," she began abruptly, in a whisper, "is the rudest, most ill-bred person I ever met. When I talked to him the" other day I thought he was nice. He was nice, But he has behaved abominably - like a boor - like a sulky child. Has he no sense of humor? Because I played a joke on him, is that any reason why he should hurt me?"

"Hurt you?" exclaimed little Holworthy in amazement. "Don't be ridiculous! How could he hurt you? Why should you care how rude he is? Ward's a clever fellow, but he fancies himself. He's conceited. He's too good-looking; and a lot of silly women have made such a fuss over him. So when one of them laughs at him he can't understand it. That's the trouble. I could see that when I was telling him."

"Telling him!" repeated Miss Flagg - "Telling him what?"

"About what a funny story you made of it," explained Holworthy. "About his having the nerve to ask you to feed the monkeys and to lunch with him."

Miss Flagg interrupted with a gasping intake of her breath.

"Oh!" she said softly. "So-so you told him that, did you? And - what else did you tell him?" ,

"Only what you told us - that he said 'the day could not begin too soon'; that he said he wouldn't let you be a manicure and wash the hands of men who weren't fit to wash the streets you walked on."

There was a pause.

"Did I tell you he said that?" breathed Anita Flagg.

"You know you did," said Holworthy.

There was another pause.

"I must have been mad!" said the girl.

There was a longer pause and Holworthy shifted uneasily.

"I'm afraid you are angry," he ventured.

"Angry!" exclaimed Miss Flagg. "I should say I was angry, but not with you. I'm very much pleased with you. At the end of the act I'm going to let you take me out into the lobby."

With his arms tightly folded, Sam sat staring unhappily at the stage and seeing nothing. He was sorry for himself because Anita Flagg had destroyed his ideal of a sweet and noble woman - and he was sorry for Miss Flagg because a man had been rude to her. That he happened to be that man did not make his sorrow and indignation the less intense; and, indeed, so miserable was he and so miserable were his looks, that his friends on the stage considered sending him a note, offering, if he would take himself out of the front row, to give him back his money at the box office. Sam certainly wished to take himself away; but he did not want to admit that he was miserable, that he had behaved ill, that the presence of Anita Flagg could spoil his evening - could, in the slightest degree affect him. So he sat, completely wretched, feeling that he was in a false position; that if he were it was his own fault; that he had acted like an ass and a brute. It was not a cheerful feeling.

When the curtain fell he still remained seated. He knew before the second act there was an interminable wait; but he did not want to chance running into Holworthy in the lobby and he told himself it would be rude to abandon Sister Anne. But he now was not so conscious of the imaginary Sister Anne as of the actual box party on his near right, who were laughing and chattering volubly. He wondered whether they laughed at him - whether Miss Flagg were again entertaining them at his expense; again making his advances appear ridiculous. He was so sure of it that he flushed indignantly. He was glad he had been rude.

And then, at his elbow, there was the rustle of silk; and a beautiful figure, all in black velvet, towered above him, then crowded past him, and sank into the empty seat at his side. He was too startled to speak - and Miss Anita Flagg seemed to understand that and to wish to give him time; for, without regarding him in the least, and as though to establish the fact that she had come to stay, she began calmly and deliberately to remove the bell-like hat. This accomplished, she bent toward him, her eyes looking straight into his, her smile reproaching him. In the familiar tone of an old and dear friend she said to him gently:

"This is the day you planned for me. Don't you think you've wasted quite enough of it?"

Sam looked back into the eyes, and saw in them no trace of laughter or of mockery, but, instead, gentle reproof and appeal - and something else that, in turn, begged of him to be gentle.

For a moment, too disturbed to speak, he looked at her, miserably, remorsefully.

"It's not Anita Flagg at all," he said. "It's Sister Anne come back to life again!" The girl shook her head.

"No; it's Anita Flagg. I'm not a bit like the girl you thought you met and I did say all the, things Holworthy told you I said; but that was before I understood - before I read what you wrote about Sister Anne - about the kind of me you thought you'd met. When I read that I knew what sort of a man you were. I knew you had been really kind and gentle, and I knew you had dug out something that I did not know was there - that no one else had found. And I remembered how you called me Sister. I mean the way you said it. And I wanted to hear it again. I wanted you to say it."

She lifted her face to his. She was very near him - so near that her shoulder brushed against his arm. In the box above them her friends, scandalized and amused, were watching her with the greatest interest. Half of the people in the now half-empty house were watching them with the greatest interest. To them, between reading advertisements on the programme and watching Anita Flagg making desperate love to a lucky youth in the front row, there was no question of which to choose.

The young people in the front row did not know they were observed. They were alone - as much alone as though they were seated in a biplane, sweeping above the clouds.

"Say it again," prompted Anita Flagg "Sister."

"I will not!" returned the young man firmly. "But I'll say this," he whispered: "I'll say you're the most wonderful, the most beautiful, and the finest woman who has ever lived!"

Anita Flagg's eyes left his quickly; and, with her head bent, she stared at the bass drum in the orchestra.

"I don't know," she said, "but that sounds just as good."

When the curtain was about to rise she told him to take

her back to her box, so that he could meet her friends and go on with them to supper; but when they reached the rear of the house she halted.

"We can see this act," she said, "or - my car's in front of the theatre - we might go to the park and take a turn or two or three. Which would you prefer?"

"Don't make me laugh!" said Sam.

As they sat all together at supper with those of the box party, but paying no attention to them whatsoever, Anita Flagg sighed contentedly.

"There's only one thing," she said to Sam, "that is making me unhappy; and because it is such sad news I haven't told you.

It is this: I am leaving America. I am going to spend the winter in London. I sail next Wednesday."

"My business is to gather news," said Sam, but in all my life I never gathered such good news as that."

"Good news!" exclaimed Anita.

"Because," explained Sam, "I am leaving, America - am spending the winter in England. I am sailing on Wednesday. No; I also am unhappy; but that is not what makes me unhappy."

"Tell me," begged Anita.

"Some day," said Sam.

The day he chose to tell her was the first day they were

at sea - as they leaned upon the rail, watching Fire Island disappear.

"This is my unhappiness," said Sam - and he pointed to a name on the passenger list. It was: "The Earl of Deptford, and valet." "And because he is on board!"

Anita Flagg gazed with interest at a pursuing sea-gull.

"He is not on board," she said. "He changed to another boat."

Sam felt that by a word from her a great weight might be lifted from his soul. He looked at her appealingly - hungrily.

"Why did he change?" he begged.

Anita Flagg shook her head in wonder. She smiled at him with amused despair.

"Is that all that is worrying you?" she said.

Chapter 2.

THE GRAND CROSS OF THE CRESCENT

Of some college students it has been said that, in order to pass their examinations, they will deceive and cheat their kind professors. This may or may not be true. One only can shudder and pass hurriedly on. But whatever others may have done, when young Peter Hallowell in his senior year came up for those final examinations which, should he pass them even by a nose, would gain him his degree, he did not cheat. He may have been too honest, too confident, too lazy, but Peter did not cheat. It was the professors who cheated.

At Stillwater College, on each subject on which you are examined you can score a possible hundred. That means perfection, and in, the brief history of Stillwater, which is a very, new college, only one man has attained it. After graduating he "accepted a position" in an asylum for the insane, from which he was, promoted later to the poor-house, where he died. Many Stillwater undergraduates studied his career and, lest they also should attain perfection, were afraid to study anything else. Among these Peter was by far the most afraid.

The marking system at Stillwater is as follows: If in all the subjects in which you have been examined your marks added together give you an average of ninety, you are passed "with honors"; if of seventy-five, you pass "with distinction"; if Of fifty, You just "pass." It is not unlike the grocer's nice adjustment of fresh eggs, good eggs, and eggs. The whole college knew that if Peter got in among the eggs he would be lucky, but the professors and instructors of Stillwater 'were determined that, no matter what young Hallowell might do to prevent it, they would see that he passed his examinations. And they constituted the jury of awards. Their interest in Peter was not because they loved him so much, but because each loved his own vine-covered cottage, his salary, and his dignified title the more. And each knew that that one of the faculty who dared to flunk the son of old man Hallowell, who had endowed Stillwater, who supported Stillwater, and who might be expected to go on supporting Stillwater indefinitely, might also at the same time hand in his official resignation.

Chancellor Black, the head of Stillwater, was an up-to-date college president. If he did not actually run after money he went where money was, and it was not his habit to be downright rude to those who possessed it. And if any three-thousand-dollar-a-year professor, through a too strict respect for Stillwater's standards of learning, should lose to that institution a half-million-dollar observatory, swimming-pool, or gymnasium, he was the sort of college president, who would see to it that the college lost also the services of that too conscientious instructor.

He did not put this in writing or in words, but just before the June examinations, when on, the campus he met one of the faculty, he would inquire with kindly interest as to the standing of young Hallowell.

"That is too bad!" he would exclaim, but, more in sorrow than in anger. "Still, I hope the boy can pull through. He is his dear father's pride, and his father's heart is set upon his son's obtaining his degree. Let us hope he will pull through." For four years every professor had been pulling Peter through, and the conscience of each had become calloused. They had only once more to shove him through and they would be free of him forever. And so, although they did not conspire together, each knew that of the firing squad that was to aim its rifles at, Peter, HIS rifle would hold the blank cartridge.

The only one of them who did not know this was Doctor Henry Gilman. Doctor Gilman was the professor of ancient and modern history at Stillwater, and greatly respected and loved. He also was the author of those well-known text-books, "The Founders of Islam," and "The Rise and Fall of the Turkish Empire." This latter work, in five volumes, had been not unfavorably compared to Gibbon's "Decline and Fall of the Roman Empire." The original newspaper comment, dated some thirty years back, the doctor had preserved, and would produce it, now somewhat frayed and worn, and read it to visitors. He knew it by heart, but to him it always possessed a contemporary and news interest.

"Here is a review of the history," he would say - he always referred to it as "the" history - "that I came across in my TRANSCRIPT."

In the eyes of Doctor Gilman thirty years was so brief a period that it was as though the clipping had been printed the previous after-noon.

The members of his class who were examined on the "Rise and Fall," and who invariably came to grief over it, referred to it briefly as the Fall," sometimes feelingly as "the. . . .Fall." The" history began when Constantinople was Byzantium, skipped lightly over six centuries to Constantine, and in the last two Volumes finished up the Mohammeds with the downfall of the fourth one and the coming of Suleiman. Since Suleiman, Doctor Gilman did not recognize Turkey as being on the map. When his history said the Turkish Empire had fallen, then the Turkish Empire fell. Once Chancellor Black suggested that he add a sixth volume that would cover the last three centuries.

"In a history of Turkey issued as a text-book," said the chancellor, "I think the Russian-Turkish War should be included."

Doctor Gilman, from behind his gold-rimmed spectacles, gazed at him in mild reproach. "The war in the Crimea!" he exclaimed. "Why, I was alive at the time. I know about it. That is not history."

Accordingly, it followed that to a man who since the seventeenth century knew of no event, of interest, Cyrus Hallowell, of the meat-packers' trust, was not an imposing figure. And such a man the son of Cyrus Hallowell was but an ignorant young savage, to whom "the" history certainly had been a closed book. And so when Peter returned his examination paper in a condition almost as spotless as that in which he had received it, Doctor Gilman carefully and conscientiously, with malice toward none and, with no thought of the morrow, marked" five."

Each of the other professors and instructors had marked Peter fifty. In their fear of Chancellor Black they dared not give the boy less, but they refused to be slaves to the extent of crediting him with a single point higher than was necessary to pass him. But Doctor Gilman's five completely knocked out the required average of fifty, and young Peter was "found" and could not graduate. It was an awful business! The only son of the only Hallowell refused a degree in his father's own private college - the son of the man who had built the Hallowell Memorial, the new Laboratory, the Anna Hallowell Chapel, the Hallowell Dormitory, and the Hallowell Athletic Field. When on the bulletin board of the dim hall of the Memorial to his departed grandfather Peter read of his own disgrace and downfall, the light the stained-glass window cast upon his nose was of no sicklier a green than was the nose itself. Not that Peter wanted an A.M. or an A.B., not that he desired laurels he had not won, but because the young man was afraid of his father. And he had cause to be. Father arrived at Stillwater the next morning. The interviews that followed made Stillwater history.

"My son is not an ass!" is what Hallowell senior is said to have said to Doctor Black. "And if in four years you and your faculty cannot give him the rudiments of an education, I will send him to a college that can. And I'll send my money where I send Peter."

In reply Chancellor Black could have said that it was the fault of the son and not of the college; he could have said that where three men had failed to graduate one hundred and eighty had not. But did he say that? Oh, no, he did not say that! He was not that sort of, a college president. Instead, he remained calm and sympathetic, and like a conspirator in a comic opera glanced apprehensively round his, study. He lowered his voice.

"There has been contemptible work here, "he whispered - "spite and a mean spirit of reprisal. I have been making a secret investigation, and I find that this blow at your son and you, and at the good name of our college was struck by one man, a man with a grievance - Doctor Gilman. Doctor Gilman has repeatedly desired me to raise his salary." This did not happen to be true, but in such a crisis Dotor Black could not afford to be too particular.

"I have seen no reason for raising his salary - and there you have the explanation. In revenge he has made this attack. But he overshot his mark. In causing us temporary embarrassment he has brought about his own downfall. I have already asked for his resignation."

Every day in the week Hallowell was a fair, sane man, but on this particular day he was wounded, his spirit was hurt, his self-esteem humiliated. He was in a state of mind to believe anything rather than that his son was an idiot.

"I don't want the man discharged," he protested, "just because Peter is lazy. But if Doctor Gilman was moved by personal considerations, if he sacrificed my Peter in order to get even . . . ."

"That," exclaimed Black in a horrified whisper, "is exactly what he did! Your generosity to the college is well known. You are recognized all over America as its patron. And he believed that when I refused him an increase in salary it was really you who refused it - and he struck at you through your son. Everybody thinks so. The college is on fire with indignation. And look at the mark he gave Peter! Five! That in itself shows the malice. Five is not a mark, it is an insult! No one, certainly not your brilliant son - look how brilliantly he managed the glee-club and foot-ball tour - is stupid enough to deserve five. No, Doctor Gilman went too far. And he has been justly punished!"

What Hallowell senior was willing to believe of what the chancellor told him, and his opinion of the matter as expressed to Peter, differed materially.

"They tell me," he concluded, "that in the fall they will give you another examination, and if you pass then, you will get your degree. No one will know you've got it. They'll slip it to you out of the side-door like a cold potato to a tramp. The only thing people will know is that when your classmates stood up and got their parchments - the thing they'd been working for four years, the only reason for their going to college at all - YOU were not among those present. That's your fault; but if you don't get your degree next fall that will be my fault. I've supported you through college and you've failed to deliver the goods. Now you deliver them next fall, or you can support yourself."

"That will be all right," said Peter humbly; "I'll pass next fall."

"I'm going to make sure of that," said Hallowell senior. "To-morrow you will take those history books that you did not open, especially Gilman's 'Rise and Fall,' which it seems you have not even purchased, and you will travel for the entire summer with a private tutor . . . ."

Peter, who had personally conducted the foot-ball and base-ball teams over half of the Middle States and daily bullied and browbeat them, protested with indignation. "WON'T travel with a private tutor!"

"If I say so," returned Hallowell senior grimly, "you'll travel with a governess and a trained nurse, and wear a strait jacket. And you'll continue to wear it until you can recite the history of Turkey backward. And in order that you may know it backward - and forward you will spend this summer in Turkey - in Constantinople - until I send you permission to come home."

"Constantinople!" yelled Peter. "In August! Are you serious?"

" Do I look it?" asked Peter's father. He did.

"In Constantinople," explained Mr. Hallowell senior, "there will be nothing to distract you from your studies, and in spite of yourself every minute you will be imbibing history and local color."

"I'll be imbibing fever,", returned Peter, "and sunstroke and sudden death. If you want to get rid of me, why don't you send me to the island where they sent Dreyfus? It's quicker. You don't have to go to Turkey to study about Turkey."

"You do!" said his father.

Peter did not wait for the festivities of commencement week. All day he hid in his room, packing his belongings or giving them away to e members of his class, who came to tell him what a rotten shame it was, and to bid him good-by. They loved Peter for himself alone, and at losing him were loyally enraged. They sired publicly to express their sentiments, and to that end they planned a mock trial of the Rise and Fall," at which a packed jury would sentence it to cremation. They planned also to hang Doctor Gilman in effigy. The effigy with a rope round its neck was even then awaiting mob violence. It was complete to the silver-white beard and the gold spectacles. But Peter squashed both demonstrations. He did not know Doctor Gilman had been forced to resign, but he protested that the horse-play of his friends would make him appear a bad loser. "It would look, boys," he said, "as though I couldn't take my medicine. Looks like kicking against the umpire's decision. Old Gilman fought fair. He gave me just what was coming to me. I think a darn sight more of him than do of that bunch of boot-lickers that had the colossal nerve to pretend I scored fifty!"

Doctor Gilman sat in his cottage that stood the edge of the campus, gazing at a plaster bust of Socrates which he did not see. Since that morning he had ceased to sit in the chair of history at Stillwater College. They were retrenching, the chancellor had told him curtly, cutting down unnecessary expenses, for even in his anger Doctor Black was too intelligent to hint at his real motive, and the professor was far too innocent of evil, far too detached from college politics to suspect. He would remain a professor emeritus on half pay, but he no longer would teach. The college he had served for thirty years-since it consisted of two brick buildings and a faculty of ten young men - no longer needed him. Even his ivy-covered cottage, in which his wife and he had lived for twenty years, in which their one child had died, would at the beginning of the next term be required of him. But the college would allow him those six months in which to "look round." So, just outside the circle of light from his student lamp, he sat in his study, and stared with unseeing eyes at the bust of Socrates. He was not considering ways and means. They must be faced later. He was considering how he could possibly break the blow to his wife. What eviction from that house would mean to her no one but he understood. Since the day their little girl had died, nothing in the room that had been her playroom, bedroom, and nursery had been altered, nothing had been touched. To his wife, somewhere in the house that wonderful, God-given child was still with them. Not as a memory but as a real and living presence. When at night the professor and his wife sat at either end of the study table, reading by the same lamp, he would see her suddenly lift her head, alert and eager, as though from the nursery floor a step had sounded, as though from the darkness a sleepy voice had called her. And when they would be forced to move to lodgings in the town, to some students' boarding-house, though they could take with them their books, their furniture, their mutual love and comradeship, they must leave behind them the haunting presence of the child, the colored pictures she had cut from the Christmas numbers and plastered over the nursery walls, the rambler roses that with her own hands she had planted and that now climbed to her window and each summer peered into her empty room.

Outside Doctor Gilman's cottage, among the trees of the campus, paper lanterns like oranges aglow were swaying in the evening breeze. In front of Hallowell the flame of a bonfire shot to the top of the tallest elms, and gathered in a circle round it the glee club sang, and cheer succeeded cheer-cheers for the heroes of the cinder track, for the heroes of the diamond and the gridiron , cheers for the men who had flunked especially for one man who had flunked. But for that man who for thirty years in the class room had served the college there were no cheers. No one remembered him, except the one student who had best reason to remember him. But this recollection Peter had no rancor or bitterness and, still anxious lest he should be considered a bad loser, he wished Doctor Gilman a every one else to know that. So when the celebration was at its height and just before train was due to carry him from Stillwater, ran across the campus to the Gilman cottage say good-by. But he did not enter the cottage He went so far only as half-way up the garden walk. In the window of the study which opened upon the veranda he saw through frame of honeysuckles the professor and wife standing beside the study table. They were clinging to each other, the woman weep silently with her cheek on his shoulder, thin, delicate, well-bred hands clasping arms, while the man comforted her awkward unhappily, with hopeless, futile caresses.

Peter, shocked and miserable at what he had seen, backed steadily away. What disaster had befallen the old couple he could not imagine. The idea that he himself might in any way connected with their grief never entered mind. He was certain only that, whatever the trouble was, it was something so intimate and personal that no mere outsider might dare to offer his sympathy. So on tiptoe he retreated down the garden walk and, avoiding the celebration at the bonfire, returned to his rooms. An hour later the entire college escorted him to the railroad station, and with "He's a jolly good fellow" and "He's off to Philippopolis in the morn - ing" ringing in his ears, he sank back his seat in the smoking-car and gazed at the lights of Stillwater disappearing out of his life. And he was surprised to find that what lingered his mind was not the students, dancing like Indians round the bonfire, or at the steps of the smoking-car fighting to shake his hand, but the man and woman alone in the cottage stricken with sudden sorrow, standing like two children lost in the streets, who cling to each other for comfort and at the same moment whisper words of courage.

Two months Later, at Constantinople, Peter, was suffering from remorse over neglected opportunities, from prickly heat, and from fleas. And it not been for the moving-picture man, and the poker and baccarat at the Cercle Oriental, he would have flung himself into the Bosphorus. In the mornings with the tutor he read ancient history, which he promptly forgot; and for the rest of the hot, dreary day with the moving-picture man through the bazaars and along the water-front he stalked suspects for the camera.

The name of the moving-picture man was Harry Stetson. He had been a newspaper reporter, a press-agent, and an actor in vaudeville and in a moving-picture company. Now on his own account he was preparing an illustrated lecture on the East, adapted to churches and Sunday-schools. Peter and he wrote it in collaboration, and in the evenings rehearsed it with lantern slides before an audience of the hotel clerk, the tutor, and the German soldier of fortune who was trying to sell the young Turks very old battleships. Every other foreigner had fled the city, and the entire diplomatic corps had removed itself to the summer capital at Therapia.

There Stimson, the first secretary of the embassy and,

in the absence of the ambassador, CHARGE D'AFFAIRES, invited Peter to become his guest. Stimson was most anxious to be polite to Peter, for Hallowell senior was a power in the party then in office, and a word from him at Washington in favor of a rising young diplomat would do no harm. But Peter was afraid his father would consider Therapia "out of bounds."

"He sent me to Constantinople," explained Peter, "and if he thinks I'm not playing the game the Lord only knows where he might send me next-and he might cut off my allowance."

In the matter of allowance Peter's father had been most generous. This was fortunate, for poker, as the pashas and princes played it at he Cercle, was no game for cripples or children. But, owing to his letter-of-credit and his illspent life, Peter was able to hold his own against men three times his age and of fortunes nearly equal to that of his father. Only they disposed of their wealth differently. On many hot evening Peter saw as much of their money scattered over the green table as his father had spent over the Hallowell athletic field.

In this fashion Peter spent his first month of exile - in the morning trying to fill his brain with names of great men who had been a long time dead, and in his leisure hours with local color. To a youth of his active spirit it was a full life without joy or recompense. A Letter from Charley Hines, a classmate who lived at Stillwater, which arrived after Peter had endured six weeks of Constantinople, released him from boredom and gave life a real interest. It was a letter full of gossip intended to amuse. One paragraph failed of its purpose. It read: "Old man Gilman has got the sack.

The chancellor offered him up as a sacrifice to your father, and because he was unwise enough to flunk you. He is to move out in September. I ran across them last week when I was looking for rooms for a Freshman cousin. They were reserving one in the same boarding-house. It's a shame, and I know you'll agree. They are a fine old couple, and I don't like to think of them herding with Freshmen in a shine boardinghouse. Black always was a swine."

Peter spent fully ten minutes getting to the cable office.

"Just learned," he cabled his father, "Gilman dismissed because flunked me consider this outrageous please see he is reinstated."

The answer, which arrived the next day, did not satisfy Peter. It read: "Informed Gilman acted through spite have no authority as you know to interfere any act of black."

Since Peter had learned of the disaster that through his laziness had befallen the Gilmans, his indignation at the injustice had been hourly increasing. Nor had his banishment to Constantinople strengthened his filial piety. On the contrary, it had rendered him independent and but little inclined to kiss the paternal rod. In consequence his next cable was not conciliatory.

"Dismissing Gilman Looks more Like we acted through spite makes me appear contemptible Black is a toady will do as you direct please reinstate."

To this somewhat peremptory message his father answered:

"If your position unpleasant yourself to blame not Black incident is closed."

"Is it?" said the son of his father. He called Stetson to his aid and explained. Stetson reminded him of the famous cablegram of his distinguished contemporary: "Perdicaris alive and Raisuli dead!"

Peter's paraphrase of this ran: "Gilman returns to Stillwater or I will not try for degree."

The reply was equally emphatic:

"You earn your degree or you earn your own living."

This alarmed Stetson, but caused Peter to deliver his ultimatum: "Choose to earn my own living am leaving Constantinople."

Within a few days Stetson was also leaving Constantinople by steamer via Naples. Peter, who had come to like him very much, would have accompanied him had he not preferred to return home more leisurely by way of Paris and London.

"You'll get there long before I do," said Peter, "and as soon as you arrive I want you to go to Stillwater and give Doctor Gilman some souvenir of Turkey from me. Just to show him I've no hard feelings. He wouldn't accept money, but he can't refuse a present. I want it to be something characteristic of the country, Like a prayer rug, or a scimitar, or an illuminated Koran, or "

Somewhat doubtfully, somewhat sheepishly, Stetson drew from his pocket a flat morocco case and opened it. "What's the matter with one of these?" he asked.

In a velvet-lined jewel case was a star of green enamel and silver gilt. To it was attached a ribbon of red and green.

"That's the Star of the Crescent," said Peter. "Where did you buy it?"

"Buy it!" exclaimed Stetson. "You don't buy them. The Sultan bestows them."

"I'll bet the Sultan didn't bestow that one," said Peter.

"I'll bet," returned Stetson, "I've got something in my pocket that says he did."

He unfolded an imposing document covered with slanting lines of curving Arabic letters in gold. Peter was impressed but still skeptical.

"What does that say when it says it in English?" he asked.

"It says," translated Stetson, "that his Imperial Majesty, the Sultan, bestows upon Henry Stetson, educator, author, lecturer, the Star of the Order of the Crescent, of the fifth class, for services rendered to Turkey."

Peter interrupted him indignantly.

"Never try to fool the fakirs, my son," he protested. "I'm a fakir myself. What services did you ever . . . ."

"Services rendered," continued Stetson undisturbed, "in spreading throughout the United States a greater knowledge of the customs, industries, and religion of the Ottoman Empire. That," he explained, "refers to my - I should say our - moving-picture lecture. I thought it would look well if, when I lectured on Turkey, I wore a Turkish decoration, so I went after this one."

Peter regarded his young friend with incredulous admiration.

"But did they believe you," he demanded, "when you told them you were an author and educator?"

Stetson closed one eye and grinned. "They believed whatever I paid them to believe."

"If you can get one of those, "cried Peter, Old man Gilman ought to get a dozen. I'll tell them he's the author of the longest and dullest history of their flea-bitten empire that was ever written. And he's a real professor and a real author, and I can prove it. I'll show them the five volumes with his name in each. How much did that thing cost you?"

"Two hundred dollars in bribes," said Stetson briskly, "and two months of diplomacy."

"I haven't got two months for diplomacy," said Peter, "so I'll have to increase the bribes. I'll stay here and get the decoration for Gilman, and you work the papers at home. No one ever heard of the Order of the Crescent, but that only makes it the easier for us. They'll only know what we tell them, and we'll tell them it's the highest honor ever bestowed by a reigning sovereign upon an American scholar. If you tell the people often enough that anything is the best they believe you. That's the way father sells his hams. You've been a press-agent. From now on you're going to be my press-agent - I mean Doctor Gilman's press-agent. I pay your salary, but your work is to advertise him and the Order of the Crescent. I'll give you a letter to Charley Hines at Stillwater. He sends out college news to a syndicate and he's the local Associated Press man. He's sore at their discharging Gilman and he's my best friend, and he'll work the papers as far as you like. Your job is to make Stillwater College and Doctor Black and my father believe that when they lost Gilman they lost the man who made Stillwater famous. And before we get through boosting Gilman, we'll make my father's million-dollar gift laboratory look like an insult."

In the eyes of the former press-agent the light of battle burned fiercely, memories of his triumphs in exploitation, of his strategies and tactics in advertising soared before him.

"It's great!" he exclaimed. "I've got your idea and you've got me. And you're darned lucky to get me. I've been press-agent for politicians, actors, society leaders, breakfast foods, and horse-shows - and I'm the best! I was in charge of the publicity bureau for Galloway when he ran for governor. He thinks the people elected him. I know I did. Nora Nashville was getting fifty dollars a week in vaudeville when I took hold of her; now she gets a thousand. I even made people believe Mrs. Hampton-Rhodes was a society leader at Newport, when all she ever saw of Newport was Bergers and the Muschenheim-Kings. Why, I am the man that made the American People believe Russian dancers can dance!"

"It's plain to see you hate yourself," said 'Peter. "You must not get so despondent or you might commit suicide. How much money will you want?"

"How much have you got?"

"All kinds," said Peter. "Some in a letter-of-credit that my father earned from the fretful pig, and much more in cash that I won at poker from the pashas. When that's gone I've got to go to work and earn my living. Meanwhile your salary is a hundred a week and all you need to boost Gilman and the Order of the Crescent. We are now the Gilman Defense, Publicity, and Development Committee, and you will begin by introducing me to the man I am to bribe."

"In this country you don't need any introduction to the man you want to bribe," exclaimed Stetson; "you just bribe him!"

That same night in the smoking-room of the hotel, Peter and Stetson made their first move in the game of winning for Professor Gilman the Order of the Crescent. Stetson presented Peter to a young effendi in a frock coat and fez. Stetson called him Osman. He was a clerk in the foreign office and appeared to be "a friend of a friend of a friend" of the assistant third secretary.

The five volumes of the "Rise and Fall" were spread before him, and Peter demanded to know why so distinguished a scholar as Doctor Gilman had not received some recognition from the country he had so sympathetically described. Osman fingered the volumes doubtfully, and promised the matter should be brought at once to the attention of the grand vizier .

After he had departed Stetson explained that Osman

had just as little chance of getting within speaking distance of the grand vizier as of the ladies of his harem.

"It's like Tammany," said Stetson; "there are sachems, district leaders, and lieutenants. Each of them is entitled to trade or give away a few of these decorations, just as each district leader gets his percentage of jobs in the streetcleaning department. This fellow will go to his patron, his patron will go to some undersecretary in the cabinet, he will put it up to a palace favorite, and they will divide your money.

"In time the minister of foreign affairs will sign your brevet and a hundred others, without knowing what he is signing; then you cable me, and the Star of the Crescent will burst upon the United States in a way that will make Halley's comet look like a wax match."

The next day Stetson and the tutor sailed for home and Peter was left alone to pursue, as he supposed, the Order of the Crescent. On the contrary, he found that the Order of the Crescent was pursuing him. He had not appreciated that, from underlings and backstair politicians, an itinerant showman like Stetson and the only son of an American Croesus would receive very different treatment.

Within twenty-four hours a fat man with a blue-black beard and diamond rings called with Osman to apologize for the latter. Osman, the fat man explained - had been about to make a fatal error. For Doctor Gilman he had asked the Order of the Crescent of the fifth class, the same class that had been given Stetson. The fifth class, the fat man explained, was all very well for tradesmen, dragomans, and eunuchs, but as an honor for a savant as distinguished as the friend of his. Hallowell, the fourth class would hardly be high enough. The fees, the fat man added, would Also be higher; but, he pointed out, it was worth the difference, because the fourth class entitled the wearer to a salute from all sentries.

"There are few sentries at Stillwater," said Peter; "but I want the best and I want it quick. Get me the fourth class."

The next morning he was surprised by an early visit from Stimson of the embassy. The secretary was considerably annoyed.

"My dear Hallowell," he protested, "why the devil didn't you tell me you wanted a decoration? Of course the State department expressly forbids us to ask for one for ourselves, or for any one else. But what's the Constitution between friends ? I'll get it for you at once - but, on two conditions: that you don't tell anybody I got it, and that you tell me why you want it, and what you ever did to deserve it."

Instead, Peter explained fully and so sympathetically that the diplomat demanded that he, too, should be enrolled as one of the Gilman Defense Committee.

"Doctor Gilman's history," he said, "must be presented to the Sultan. You must have the five volumes rebound in red and green, the colors of Mohammed, and with as much gold tooling as they can carry. I hope," he added, they are not soiled."

"Not by me," Peter assured him.

"I will take them myself," continued Stimson, "to Muley Pasha, the minister of foreign affairs, and ask him to present them to his Imperial Majesty. He will promise to do so, but he won't; but he knows I know he won't so that is all right. And in return he will present us with the Order of the Crescent of the third class."

"Going up!" exclaimed Peter. "The third class. That will cost me my entire letter-of-credit."

"Not at all," said Stimson. "I've saved you from the grafters. It will cost you only what you pay to have the books rebound. And the THIRD class is a real honor of which any one might be proud. You wear it round your neck, and at your funeral it entitles you to an escort of a thousand soldiers."

"I'd rather put up with fewer soldiers," said Peter, " and wear it longer round my neck What's the matter with our getting the second class or the first class?"

At such ignorance Stimson could not repress a smile.

"The first class," he explained patiently, "is the Great Grand Cross, and is given only to reigning sovereigns. The second is called the Grand Cross, and is bestowed only on crowned princes, prime ministers, and men of world-wide fame . . . . "

"What's the matter with Doctor Gilman's being of world-wide fame?" said Peter. "He will be some day, when Stetson starts boosting."

"Some day," retorted Stimson stiffly, " I may be an ambassador. When I am I hope to get the Grand Cross of the Crescent, but not now. I'm sorry you're not satisfied," he added aggrievedly. "No one can get you anything higher than the third class, and I may lose my official head asking for that."

"Nothing is too good for old man Gilman," said Peter, "nor for you. You get the third class for him, and I'll have father make you an ambassador."

That night at poker at the club Peter sat next to Prince Abdul, who had come from a reception at the Grand vizier 's and still wore his decorations. Decorations now fascinated Peter, and those on the coat of the young prince he regarded with wide-eyed awe. He also regarded Abdul with wide-eyed awe, because he was the favorite nephew of the Sultan, and because he enjoyed the reputation of having the worst reputation in Turkey. Peter wondered why. He always had found Abdul charming, distinguished, courteous to the verge of humility, most cleverly cynical, most brilliantly amusing. At poker he almost invariably won, and while doing so was so politely bored, so indifferent to his cards and the cards held by others, that Peter declared he had never met his equal.

In a pause in the game, while some one tore the cover off a fresh pack, Peter pointed at the star of diamonds that nestled behind the lapel of Abdul's coat.

"May I ask what that is?" said Peter.

The prince frowned at his diamond sunburst as though it annoyed him, and then smiled delightedly.

"It is an order," he said in a quick aside, "bestowed only upon men of world-wide fame. I dined to-night," he explained , " with your charming compatriot, Mr.

Joseph Stimson."

"And Joe told?" said Peter.

The prince nodded. "Joe told," he repeated; "but it is all arranged. Your distinguished friend, the Sage of Stillwater, will receive the Crescent of the third class."

Peter's eyes were still fastened hungrily upon the diamond sunburst.

"Why," he demanded, "can't some one get him one like that?"

As though about to take offense the prince raised his eyebrows, and then thought better of it and smiled.

"There are only two men in all Turkey," he said, "who could do that."

"And is the Sultan the other one?" asked Peter. The prince gasped as though he had suddenly stepped beneath a cold shower, and then laughed long and silently.

"You flatter me," he murmured.

"You know you could if you liked!" whispered Peter stoutly.

Apparently Abdul did not hear him. "I will take one card," he said.

Toward two in the morning there was seventy-five thousand francs in the pot, and all save Prince Abdul and Peter had dropped out. "Will you divide?" asked the prince.

"Why should I?" said Peter. "I've got you beat now. Do you raise me or call?" The prince called and laid down a full house. Peter showed four tens.

"I will deal you one hand, double or quits," said the prince.

Over the end of his cigar Peter squinted at the great heap of mother-of-pearl counters and gold-pieces and bank-notes.

"You will pay me double what is on the table," he said, "or you quit owing me nothing."

The prince nodded.

"Go ahead," said Peter.

The prince dealt them each a hand and discarded two cards. Peter held a seven, a pair of kings, and a pair of fours. Hoping to draw another king, which might give him a three higher than the three held by Abdul, he threw away the seven and the lower pair. He caught another king. The prince showed three queens and shrugged his shoulders.

Peter, leaning toward him, spoke out of the corner of his mouth.

"I'll make you a sporting proposition," he murmured. "You owe me a hundred and fifty thousand francs. "I'll stake that against what only two men in the empire can give me."

The prince allowed his eyes to travel slowly round the circle of the table. But the puzzled glances of the other players showed that to them Peter's proposal conveyed no meaning.

The prince smiled cynically.

"For yourself?" he demanded.

"For Doctor Gilman," said Peter.

"We will cut for deal and one hand will decide," said the prince. His voice dropped to a whisper. "And no one must ever know," he warned.

Peter also could be cynical.

"Not even the Sultan," he said.

Abdul won the deal and gave himself a very good hand. But the hand he dealt Peter was the better one.

The prince was a good loser. The next afternoon the GAZETTE OFFICIALLY announced that upon Doctor Henry Gilman, professor emeritus of the University of Stillwater, U. S. A., the Sultan had been graciously pleased to confer the Grand Cross of the Order of the Crescent.

Peter flashed the great news to Stetson. The cable caught him at Quarantine. It read: "Captured Crescent, Grand Cross. Get busy."

But before Stetson could get busy the campaign of publicity had been brilliantly opened from Constantinople. Prince Abdul, although pitchforked into the Gilman Defense Committee, proved himself one of its most enthusiastic members.

"For me it becomes a case of NOBLESSE OBLIGE," he declared. "If it is worth doing at all it is worth doing well. To-day the Sultan will command that the "Rise and Fall" be translated into Arabic, and that it be placed in the national library. Moreover, the University of Constantinople, the College of Salonica, and the National Historical Society have each elected Doctor Gilman an honorary member. I proposed him, the Patriarch of Mesopotamia seconded him. And the Turkish ambassador in America has been instructed to present the insignia with his own hands."

Nor was Peter or Stimson idle. To assist Stetson in his press-work, and to further the idea that all Europe was now clamoring for the "Rise and fall," Peter paid an impecunious but over-educated dragoman to translate it into five languages, and Stimson officially wrote of this, and of the bestowal of the Crescent to the State Department. He pointed out that not since General Grant had passed through Europe had the Sultan so highly honored an American. He added he had been requested by the grand vizier - who had been requested by Prince Abdul - to request the State Department to inform Doctor Gilman of these high honors. A request from such a source was a command and, as desired, the State Department wrote as requested by the grand vizier to Doctor Gilman, and tendered congratulations. The fact was sent out briefly from Washington by Associated Press. This official recognition by the Government and by the newspapers was all and more than Stetson wanted. He took off his coat and with a megaphone, rather than a pen, told the people of the United States who Doctor Gilman was, who the Sultan was, what a Grand Cross was, and why America's greatest historian was not without honor save in his own country. Columns of this were paid for and appeared as "patent insides," with a portrait of Doctor Gilman taken from the STILLWATER COLLEGE ANNUAL, and a picture of the Grand Cross drawn from imagination, in eight hundred newspapers of the Middle, Western, and Eastern States. special articles, paragraphs, portraits, and pictures of the Grand Cross followed, and, using Stillwater as his base, Stetson continued to flood the country. Young Hines, the local correspondent, acting under instructions by cable from Peter, introduced him to Doctor Gilman as a traveller who lectured on Turkey, and one who was a humble admirer of the author of the "Rise and fall." Stetson, having studied it as a student crams an examination, begged that he might sit at the feet of the master. And for several evenings, actually at his feet, on the steps of the ivy-covered cottage, the disguised press-agent drew from the unworldly and unsuspecting scholar the simple story of his life. To this, still in his character as disciple and student, he added photographs he himself made of the master, of the master's ivy-covered cottage, of his favorite walk across the campus, of the great historian at work at his desk, at work in his rose garden, at play with his wife on the croquet lawn. These he held until the insignia should be actually presented. This pleasing duty fell to the Turkish ambassador, who, much to his astonishment, had received instructions to proceed to Stillwater, Massachusetts, a place of which he had never heard, and present to a Doctor Gilman, of whom he had never heard, the Grand Cross of the Crescent. As soon as the insignia arrived in the official mail-bag a secretary brought it from Washington to Boston, and the ambassador travelled down from Bar Harbor to receive it, and with the secretary took the local train to Stillwater.

The reception extended to him there is still remembered by the ambassador as one of the happiest incidents of his distinguished career. Never since he came to represent his imperial Majesty in the Western republic had its barbarians greeted him in a manner in any way so nearly approaching his own idea of what was his due.

"This ambassador," Hines had explained to the mayor of Stillwater, who was also the proprietor of its largest department store, "is the personal representative of the Sultan. So we've got to treat him right."

"It's exactly," added Stetson, "as though the Sultan himself were coming."

"And so few crowned heads visit Stillwater," continued Hines, "that we ought to show we appreciate this one, especially as he comes to pay the highest honor known to Europe to one of our townsmen."

The mayor chewed nervously on his cigar.

"What'd I better do?" he asked.

"Mr. Stetson here," Hines pointed out, "has lived in Turkey, and he knows what they expect. Maybe he will help us."

"Will you?" begged the mayor.

"I will," said Stetson.

Then they visited the college authorities. Chancellor Black and most of the faculty were on their vacations. But there were half a dozen professors still in their homes around the campus, and it was pointed out to them that the coming honor to one lately of their number reflected glory upon the college and upon them, and that they should take official action.

It was also suggested that for photographic purposes they should wear their academic robes, caps, and hoods. To these suggestions, with alacrity - partly because they all loved Doctor Gilman and partly because they had never been photographed by a moving-picture machine - they all agreed. So it came about that when the ambassador, hot and cross and dusty stepped off the way-train at Stillwater station he found to his delighted amazement a red carpet stretching to a perfectly new automobile, a company of the local militia presenting arms, a committee, consisting of the mayor in a high hat and white gloves and three professors in gowns and colored hoods, and the Stillwater silver Cornet Band playing what, after several repetitions, the ambassador was graciously pleased to recognize as his national anthem.

The ambassador forgot that he was hot and cross. He forgot that he was dusty. His face radiated satisfaction and perspiration. Here at last were people who appreciated him and his high office. And as the mayor helped him into the automobile, and those students who lived in Stillwater welcomed him with strange yells, and the moving-picture machine aimed at him point blank, he beamed with condescension. But inwardly he was ill at ease.

inwardly he was chastising himself for having, through

his ignorance of America, failed to appreciate the importance of the man he had come to honor. When he remembered he had never even heard of Doctor Gilman he blushed with confusion. And when he recollected that he had been almost on the point of refusing to come to Stillwater, that he had considered leaving the presentation to his secretary, he shuddered. What might not the Sultan have done to him! What a narrow escape!

Attracted by the band, by the sight of their fellow townsmen in khaki, by the sight of the stout gentleman in the red fez, by a tremendous liking and respect for Doctor Gilman, the entire town of Stillwater gathered outside his cottage. And inside, the old professor, trembling and bewildered and yet strangely happy, bowed his shoulders while the ambassador slipped over them the broad green scarf and upon his only frock coat pinned the diamond sunburst. In woeful embarrassment Doctor Gilman smiled and bowed and smiled, and then, as the delighted mayor of Stillwater shouted, "Speech," in sudden panic he reached out his hand quickly and covertly, and found the hand of his wife.

"Now, then, three Long ones!" yelled the cheer leader. "Now, then, 'See the Conquering Hero!'" yelled the bandmaster. "Attention! Present arms!" yelled the militia captain; and the townspeople and the professors applauded and waved their hats and handkerchiefs. And Doctor Gilman and his wife, he frightened and confused, she happy and proud, and taking it all as a matter of course, stood arm in arm in the frame of honeysuckles and bowed and bowed and bowed. And the ambassador so far unbent as to drink champagne, which appeared mysteriously in tubs of ice from the

Richard Harding Davis

rear of the ivy-covered cottage, with the mayor, with the wives of the professors, with the students, with the bandmaster. Indeed, so often did he unbend that when the perfectly new automobile conveyed him back to the Touraine, he was sleeping happily and smiling in his sleep.

Peter had arrived in America at the same time as had the insignia, but Hines and Stetson would not let him show himself in Stillwater. They were afraid if all three conspirators foregathered they might inadvertently drop some clew that would lead to suspicion and discovery.

So Peter worked from New York, and his first act was anonymously to supply his father and Chancellor Black with All the newspaper accounts of the great celebration at Stillwater. When Doctor black read them he choked. Never before had Stillwater College been brought so prominently before the public, and never before had her president been so utterly and completely ignored. And what made it worse was that he recognized that even had he been present he could not have shown his face. How could he, who had, as every one connected with the college now knew, out of spite and without cause, dismissed an old and faithful servant, join in chanting his praises. He only hoped his patron, Hallowell senior, might not hear of Gilman's triumph. But Hallowell senior heard little of anything else. At his office, at his clubs, on the golf-links, every one he met congratulated him on the high and peculiar distinction that had come to his pet college.

"You certainly have the darnedest luck in backing the right horse," exclaimed a rival pork-packer enviously. "Now if I pay a hundred thousand for a Velasquez it turns out to be a bad copy worth thirty dollars, but you pay a professor three thousand and he brings you in half a million dollars' worth of free advertising. Why, this Doctor Gilman's doing as much for your college as Doctor Osler did for Johns Hopkins or as Walter Camp does for Yale."

Mr. Hallowell received these Congratulations as gracefully as he was able, and in secret raged at Chancellor Black. Each day his rage increased. It seemed as though there would never be an end to Doctor Gilman. The stone he had rejected had become the corner-stone of Stillwater. Whenever he opened a newspaper he felt like exclaiming: "Will no one rid me of this pestilent fellow?" For the "Rise and Fall," in an edition deluxe limited to two hundred copies, was being bought up by all his book-collecting millionaire friends; a popular edition was on view in the windows of every book-shop; It was offered as a prize to subscribers to all the more sedate magazines, and the name and features of the distinguished author had become famous and familiar. Not a day passed but that some new honor, at least so the newspapers stated, was thrust upon him. Paragraphs announced that he was to be the next exchange professor to Berlin; that in May he was to lecture at the Sorbonne; that in June he was to receive a degree from Oxford.

A fresh-water college on one of the Great Lakes leaped to the front by offering him the chair of history at that seat of learning at a salary of five thousand dollars a year. Some of the honors that had been thrust upon Doctor Gilman existed only in the imagination of Peter and Stetson, but this offer happened to be genuine.

" Doctor Gilman rejected it without consideration. He

read the letter from the trustees to his wife and shook his head.

"We could not be happy away from Stillwater," he said. " We have only a month more in the cottage, but after that we still can walk past it; we can look into the garden and see the flowers she planted. We can visit the place where she lies. But if we went away we should be lonely and miserable for her, and she would be lonely for us."

Mr. Hallowell could not know why Doctor Gilman had refused to leave Stillwater; but when he read that the small Eastern college at which Doctor Gilman had graduated had offered to make him its president, his jealousy knew no bounds.

He telegraphed to Black: "Reinstate Gilman at once; offer him six thousand - offer him whatever he wants, but make him promise for no consideration to leave Stillwater he is only member faculty ever brought any credit to the college if we lose him I'll hold you responsible."

The next morning, hat in hand, smiling ingratiatingly, the Chancellor called upon Doctor Gilman and ate so much humble pie that for a week he suffered acute mental indigestion. But little did Hallowell senior care for that. He had got what he wanted. Doctor Gilman, the distinguished, was back in the faculty, and had made only one condition - that he might live until he died in the ivy-covered cottage.

Two weeks later, when Peter arrived at Stillwater to take the history examination, which, should he pass it, would give him his degree, he found on every side evidences of the "worldwide fame" he himself had created. The newsstand at the depot, the book-stores, the drugstores, the picture-shops, all spoke of Doctor Gilman; and postcards showing the ivy-covered cottage, photographs and enlargements of Doctor Gilman, advertisements of the different. editions of "the" history proclaimed his fame. Peter, fascinated by the success of his own handiwork, approached the ivy-covered cottage in a spirit almost of awe. But Mrs. Gilman welcomed him with the same kindly, sympathetic smile with which she always gave courage to the unhappy ones coming up for examinations, and Doctor Gilman's high honors in no way had spoiled his gentle courtesy.

The examination was in writing, and when Peter had handed in his papers Doctor Gilman asked him if he would prefer at once to know the result.

"I should indeed!" Peter assured him.

"Then I regret to tell you, Hallowell," said the professor, "that you have not passed. I cannot possibly give you a mark higher than five." In real sympathy the sage of Stillwater raised his eyes, but to his great astonishment he found that Peter, so far from being cast down or taking offense, was smiling delightedly, much as a fond parent might smile upon the precocious act of a beloved child.

"I am afraid," said Doctor Gilman gently, "that this summer you did not work very hard for your degree!"

Peter Laughed and picked up his hat.

"To tell you the truth, Professor," he said, "you're right

I got working for something worth while - and I forgot about the degree."

Chapter 3.

THE INVASION OF ENGLAND

This is the true inside story of the invasion of England in 1911 by the Germans, and why it failed. I got my data from Baron von Gottlieb, at the time military attaché of the German Government with the Russian army in the second Russian-Japanese War, when Russia drove Japan out of Manchuria, and reduced her to a third-rate power. He told me of his part in the invasion as we sat, after the bombardment of Tokio, on the ramparts of the Emperor's palace, watching the walls of the paper houses below us glowing and smoking like the ashes of a prairie fire.

Two years before, at the time of the invasion, von Gottlieb had been Carl Schultz, the head-waiter at the East Cliff Hotel at Cromer, and a spy.

The other end of the story came to me through Lester Ford, the London correspondent of the New York Republic. They gave me permission to tell it in any fashion I pleased, and it is here set down for the first time.

In telling the story, my conscience is not in the least disturbed, for I have yet to find any one who will believe it.

What led directly to the invasion was that some week-end guest of the East Cliff Hotel left a copy of "The Riddle of the Sands" in the coffee-room, where von Gottlieb found it; and the fact that Ford attended the Shakespeare Ball. Had neither of these events taken place, the German flag might now be flying over Buckingham Palace. And, then again, it might not.

As every German knows, "The Riddle of the Sands" is a novel written by a very clever Englishman in which is disclosed a plan for the invasion of his country. According to this plan an army of infantry was to be embarked in lighters, towed by shallow-draft, sea-going tugs, and despatched simultaneously from the seven rivers that form the Frisian Isles. From there they were to be convoyed by battle-ships two hundred and forty miles through the North Sea, and thrown upon the coast of Norfolk somewhere between the Wash and Mundesley. The fact that this coast is low-lying and bordered by sand flats which at low water are dry, that England maintains no North Sea squadron, and that her nearest naval base is at Chatham, seem to point to it as the spot best adapted for such a raid.

What von Gottlieb thought was evidenced by the fact that as soon as he read the book he mailed it to the German Ambassador in London, and under separate cover sent him a letter. In this he said: "I suggest your Excellency bring this book to the notice of a certain royal personage, and of the Strategy Board. General Bolivar said, 'When you want arms, take them from the enemy.' Does not this also follow when you want ideas?"

What the Strategy Board thought of the plan is a matter

of history. This was in 1910. A year later, during the coronation week, Lester Ford went to Clarkson's to rent a monk's robe in which to appear at the Shakespeare Ball, and while the assistant departed in search of the robe, Ford was left alone in a small room hung with full-length mirrors and shelves, and packed with the uniforms that Clarkson rents for Covent Garden balls and amateur theatricals. While waiting, Ford gratified a long, secretly cherished desire to behold himself as a military man, by trying on all the uniforms on the lower shelves; and as a result, when the assistant returned, instead of finding a young American in English clothes and a high hat, he was confronted by a German officer in a spiked helmet fighting a duel with himself in the mirror. The assistant retreated precipitately, and Ford, conscious that he appeared ridiculous, tried to turn the tables by saying, " Does a German uniform always affect a Territorial like that?"

The assistant laughed good-naturedly.

"It did give me quite a turn," he said. "It's this talk of invasion, I fancy. But for a fact, sir, if I was a Coast Guard, and you came along the beach dressed like that, I'd take a shot at you, just on the chance, anyway."

"And, quite right, too!" said Ford.

He was wondering when the invasion did come whether he would stick at his post in London and dutifully forward the news to his paper, or play truant and as a war correspondent watch the news in the making. So the words of Mr. Clarkson's assistant did not sink in. But a few weeks later young Major Bellew recalled them. Bellew was giving a dinner on the terrace of the Savoy Restaurant. His guests were his nephew, young Herbert, who was only five years younger than his uncle, and Herbert's friend Birrell, an Irishman, both in their third term at the university. After five years' service in India, Bellew had spent the last "Eights" week at Oxford, and was complaining bitterly that since his day the undergraduate had deteriorated. He had found him serious, given to study, far too well behaved. Instead of Jorrocks, he read Galsworthy; instead of "wines" he found pleasure in debating clubs where he discussed socialism. Ragging, practical jokes, ingenious hoaxes, that once were wont to set England in a roar, were a lost art. His undergraduate guests combated these charges fiercely. His criticisms they declared unjust and without intelligence.

"You're talking rot!" said his dutiful nephew. "Take Phil here, for example. I've roomed with him three years and I can testify that he has never opened a book. He never heard of Galsworthy until you spoke of him. And you can see for yourself his table manners are quite as bad as yours!"

"Worse!" assented Birrell loyally.

"And as for ragging! What rags, in your day, were as good as ours; as the Carrie Nation rag, for instance, when five hundred people sat through a temperance lecture and never guessed they were listening to a man from Balliol?"

"And the Abyssinian Ambassador rag!" cried Herbert. "What price that? When the DREADNOUGHT manned the yards for him and gave him seventeen guns. That was an Oxford rag, and carried through by

Oxford men. The country hasn't stopped laughing yet. You give us a rag!" challenged Herbert. " Make it as hard as you like; something risky, something that will make the country sit up, something that will send us all to jail, and Phil and I will put it through whether it takes one man or a dozen. Go on," he persisted, "And I bet we can get fifty volunteers right here in town and all of them undergraduates."

"Give you the idea, yes!" mocked Bellew, trying to gain time. "That's just what I say. You boys to-day are so dull. You lack initiative. It's the idea that counts. Anybody can do the acting. That's just amateur theatricals!"

"Is it!" snorted Herbert. "If you want to know what stage fright is, just go on board a British battle-ship with your face covered with burnt cork and insist on being treated like an ambassador. You'll find it's a little different from a first night with the Simla Thespians!"

Ford had no part in the debate. He had been smoking comfortably and with well-timed nods, impartially encouraging each disputant. But now he suddenly laid his cigar upon his plate, and, after glancing quickly about him, leaned eagerly forward. They were at the corner table of the terrace, and, as it was now past nine o'clock, the other diners had departed to the theatres and they were quite alone. Below them, outside the open windows, were the trees of the embankment, and beyond, the Thames, blocked to the west by the great shadows of the Houses of Parliament, lit only by the flame in the tower that showed the Lower House was still sitting.

" I'LL give you an idea for a rag," whispered Ford.

"One that is risky, that will make the country sit up, that ought to land you in Jail? Have you read 'The Riddle of the Sands'?"

Bellew and Herbert nodded; Birrell made no sign.

" Don't mind him," exclaimed Herbert impatiently. "HE never reads anything! Go on!"

"It's the book most talked about," explained Ford. "And what else is most talked about?" He answered his own question. "The landing of the Germans in Morocco and the chance of war. Now, I ask you, with that book in everybody's mind, and the war scare in everybody's mind, what would happen if German soldiers appeared to-night on the Norfolk coast just where the book says they will appear? Not one soldier, but dozens of soldiers; not in one place, but in twenty places?"

"What would happen?" roared Major Bellew loyally. "The Boy Scouts would fall out of bed and kick them into the sea!"

"Shut up!" snapped his nephew irreverently. He shook Ford by the arm. "How?" he demanded breathlessly. "How are we to do it? It would take hundreds of men."

"Two men," corrected Ford, "And a third man to drive the car. I thought it out one day at Clarkson's when I came across a lot of German uniforms. I thought of it as a newspaper story, as a trick to find out how prepared you people are to meet invasion. And when you said just now that you wanted a chance to go to jail - "

"What's your plan?" interrupted Birrell.

"We would start just before dawn - " began Ford.

"We?" demanded Herbert. "Are you in this?"

"Am I in it?" cried Ford indignantly. "It's my own private invasion! I'm letting you boys in on the ground floor. If I don't go, there won t be any invasion!"

The two pink-cheeked youths glanced at each other inquiringly and then nodded.

"We accept your services, sir," said Birrell gravely. "What's your plan?"

In astonishment Major Bellew glanced from one to the other and then slapped the table with his open palm. His voice shook with righteous indignation.

"Of all the preposterous, outrageous - Are you mad?" he demanded. "Do you suppose for one minute I will allow - "

His nephew shrugged his shoulders and, rising, pushed back his chair.

"Oh, you go to the devil!" he exclaimed cheerfully. "Come on, Ford," he said. "We'll find some place where uncle can't hear us."

Two days later a touring car carrying three young men, in the twenty-one miles between Wells and Cromer, broke down eleven times. Each time this misfortune befell them one young man scattered tools in the road and on his knees hammered ostentatiously at the tin hood; and the other two occupants of the car sauntered to the beach. There they chucked pebbles at the waves and then slowly retraced their steps. Each time the route by which they returned was different from the one by which they had set forth. Sometimes they followed the beaten path down the cliff or, as it chanced to be, across the marshes; sometimes they slid down the face of the cliff; sometimes they lost themselves behind the hedges and in the lanes of the villages. But when they again reached the car the procedure of each was alike - each produced a pencil and on the face of his "Half Inch" road map traced strange, fantastic signs.

At lunch-time they stopped at the East Cliff Hotel at Cromer and made numerous and trivial inquiries about the Cromer golf links. They had come, they volunteered, from Ely for a day of sea-bathing and golf; they were returning after dinner. The head-waiter of the East Cliff Hotel gave them the information they desired. He was an intelligent head-waiter, young, and of pleasant, not to say distinguished, bearing. In a frock coat he might easily have been mistaken for something even more important than a head-waiter - for a German riding-master, a leader of a Hungarian band, a manager of a Ritz hotel. But he was not above his station. He even assisted the porter in carrying the coats and golf bags of the gentlemen from the car to the coffee-room where, with the intuition of the homing pigeon, the three strangers had, unaided, found their way. As Carl Schultz followed, carrying the dust-coats, a road map fell from the pocket of one of them to the floor. Carl Schultz picked it up, and was about to replace it, when his eyes were held by notes scrawled roughly in pencil. With an expression that no longer was that of a head-waiter, Carl cast one swift glance about him and then slipped into the empty coat-room and locked the door. Five minutes later, with a smile that played uneasily over a face grown gray with anxiety, Carl presented the map to the tallest of the three strangers. It was open so that the pencil marks were most obvious. By his accent it was evident the tallest of the three strangers was an American.

"What the devil!" he protested; "which of you boys has been playing hob with my map?"

For just an instant the two pink-cheeked ones regarded him with disfavor; until, for just an instant, his eyebrows rose and, with a glance, he signified the waiter.

"Oh, that!" exclaimed the younger one. "The Automobile Club asked us to mark down petrol stations. Those marks mean that's where you can buy petrol."

The head-waiter breathed deeply. With an assured and happy countenance, he departed and, for the two-hundredth time that day, looked from the windows of the dining-room out over the tumbling breakers to the gray stretch of sea. As though fearful that his face would expose his secret, he glanced carefully about him and then, assured he was alone, leaned eagerly forward, scanning the empty, tossing waters.

In his mind's eye he beheld rolling tug-boats straining against long lines of scows, against the dead weight of field-guns, against the pull of thousands of motionless, silent figures, each in khaki, each in a black leather helmet, each with one hundred and fifty rounds.

In his own language Carl Schultz reproved himself.

"Patience," he muttered; "patience! By ten to-night all will be dark. There will be no stars. There will be no moon. The very heavens fight for us, and by sunrise our outposts will be twenty miles inland!"

At lunch-time Carl Schultz carefully, obsequiously waited upon the three strangers. He gave them their choice of soup, thick or clear, of gooseberry pie or Half-Pay pudding. He accepted their shillings gratefully, and when they departed for the links he bowed them on their way. And as their car turned up Jetty Street, for one instant, he again allowed his eyes to sweep the dull gray ocean. Brown-sailed fishing-boats were beating in toward Cromer. On the horizon line a Norwegian tramp was drawing a lengthening scarf of smoke. Save for these the sea was empty.

By gracious permission of the manageress Carl had obtained an afternoon off, and, changing his coat, he mounted his bicycle and set forth toward Overstrand. On his way he nodded to the local constable, to the postman on his rounds, to the driver of the char à banc. He had been a year in Cromer and was well known and well liked.

Three miles from Cromer, at the top of the highest hill in Overstrand, the chimneys of a house showed above a thick tangle of fir-trees. Between the trees and the road rose a wall, high, compact, forbidding. Carl opened the gate in the wall and pushed his bicycle up a winding path hemmed in by bushes. At the sound of his feet on the gravel the bushes new apart, and a man sprang into the walk and confronted him. But, at sight of the head-waiter, the legs of the man became rigid, his heels clicked together, his hand went sharply to his visor.

Behind the house, surrounded on every side by trees, was a tiny lawn. In the centre of the lawn, where once had been a tennis court, there now stood a slim mast. From this mast dangled tiny wires that ran to a kitchen table. On the table, its brass work shining in the sun, was a new and perfectly good wireless outfit, and beside it, with his hand on the key, was a heavily built, heavily bearded German. In his turn, Carl drew his legs together, his heels clicked, his hand stuck to his visor.

"I have been in constant communication," said the man with the beard. "They will be here just before the dawn. Return to Cromer vand openly from the post-office telegraph your cousin in London: 'Will meet you to-morrow at the Crystal Palace.' On receipt of that, in the last edition of all of this afternoon's papers, he will insert the final advertisement. Thirty thousand of our own people will read it. They will know the moment has come!"

As Carl coasted back to Cromer he flashed past many pretty gardens where, upon the lawns, men in flannels were busy at tennis or, with pretty ladies, deeply occupied in drinking tea. Carl smiled grimly. High above him on the sky-line of the cliff he saw the three strangers he had served at luncheon. They were driving before them three innocuous golf balls.

"A nation of wasters," muttered the German, "sleeping at their posts. They are fiddling while England falls!"

Mr. Shutliffe, of Stiffkey, had led his cow in from the marsh, and was about to close the cow-barn door, when three soldiers appeared suddenly around the wall of the village church. They ran directly toward him. It was nine o'clock, but the twilight still held. The uniforms the men wore were unfamiliar, but in his day Mr. Shutliffe had seen many uniforms, and to him all uniforms looked alike. The tallest soldier snapped at Mr. Shutliffe fiercely in a strange tongue.

"Du bist gefangen!" he announced. "Das Dorf ist besetzt. Wo sind unsere Leute?" he demanded.

"You'll 'ave to excuse me, sir," said Mr. Shutliffe, "but I am a trifle 'ard of 'earing."

The soldier addressed him in English.

"What is the name of this village?" he demanded.

Mr. Shuttiffe, having lived in the village upward of eighty years, recalled its name with difficulty.

"Have you seen any of our people?"

With another painful effort of memory Mr. Shutliffe shook his head.

"Go indoors!" commanded the soldier, "And put out all lights, and remain indoors. We have taken this village. We are Germans. You are a prisoner! Do you understand?"

"Yes, sir, thank'ee, sir, kindly," stammered Mr. Shutliffe. "May I lock in the pigs first, sir?"

One of the soldiers coughed explosively, and ran away, and the two others trotted after him. When they looked back, Mr. Shutliffe was still standing uncertainly in the dusk, mildly concerned as to whether he should lock up the pigs or obey the German gentleman.

The three soldiers halted behind the church wall.

"That was a fine start!" mocked Herbert. "Of course, you had to pick out the Village Idiot. If they are all going to take it like that, we had better pack up and go home."

"The village inn is still open," said Ford. "We'll close It."

They entered with fixed bayonets and dropped the butts of their rifles on the sanded floor. A man in gaiters choked over his ale and two fishermen removed their clay pipes and stared. The bar-maid alone arose to the occasion.

"Now, then," she exclaimed briskly, "What way is that to come tumbling into a respectable place? None of your tea-garden tricks in here, young fellow, my lad, or - "

The tallest of the three intruders, in deep guttural accents, interrupted her sharply.

"We are Germans!" he declared. "This village is captured. You are prisoners of war. Those lights you will out put, and yourselves lock in. If you into the street go, we will shoot!"

He gave a command in a strange language; so strange, indeed, that the soldiers with him failed to entirely grasp his meaning, and one shouldered his rifle, while the other brought his politely to a salute.

"You ass!" muttered the tall German. " Get out!"

As they charged into the street, they heard behind them a wild feminine shriek, then a crash of pottery and glass, then silence, and an instant later the Ship Inn was buried in darkness.

"That will hold Stiffkey for a while!" said Ford. "Now, back to the car."

But between them and the car loomed suddenly a tall and impressive figure. His helmet and his measured tread upon the deserted cobble-stones proclaimed his calling.

"The constable!" whispered Herbert. "He must see us, but he mustn't speak to us."

For a moment the three men showed themselves in the middle of the street, and then, as though at sight of the policeman they had taken alarm, disappeared through an opening between two houses. Five minutes later a motor-car, with its canvas top concealing its occupants, rode slowly into Stiffkey's main street and halted before the constable. The driver of the car wore a leather skull-cap and goggles. From his neck to his heels he was covered by a raincoat.

"Mr. Policeman," he began; " when I turned in here three soldiers stepped in front of my car and pointed rifles at me. Then they ran off toward the beach. What's the idea - manoeuvres? Because, they've no right to - "

"Yes, sir," the policeman assured him promptly; "I saw them. It's manoeuvres, sir. Territorials."

"They didn't look like Territorials," objected the chauffeur. "They looked like Germans."

Protected by the deepening dusk, the constable made no effort to conceal a grin.

"Just Territorials, sir," he protested soothingly; "skylarking maybe, but meaning no harm. Still, I'll have a look round, and warn 'em."

A voice from beneath the canvas broke in angrily:

"I tell you, they were Germans. It's either a silly joke, or it's serious, and you ought to report it. It's your duty to warn the Coast Guard."

The constable considered deeply.

"I wouldn't take it on myself to wake the Coast Guard," he protested; "not at this time of the night. But if any Germans' been annoying you, gentlemen, and you wish to lodge a complaint against them, you give me your cards - "

"Ye gods!" cried the man in the rear of the car. "Go on!" he commanded.

As the car sped out of Stiffkey, Herbert exclaimed with disgust:

"What's the use!" he protested. "You couldn't wake these people with dynamite! I vote we chuck it and go home."

"They little know of England who only Stiffkey know," chanted the chauffeur reprovingly. "Why, we haven't begun yet. Wait till we meet a live wire!"

Two miles farther along the road to Cromer, young Bradshaw, the job-master's son at Blakeney, was leading his bicycle up the hill. Ahead of him something heavy flopped from the bank into the road - and in the light of his acetylene lamp he saw a soldier. The soldier dodged across the road and scrambled through the hedge on the bank opposite. He was followed by another soldier, and then by a third. The last man halted.

"Put out that light," he commanded. " Go to your home and tell no one what you have seen. If you attempt to give an alarm you will be shot. Our sentries are placed every fifty yards along this road."

The soldier disappeared from in front of the ray of light and followed his comrades, and an instant later young Bradshaw heard them sliding over the cliff's edge and the pebbles clattering to the beach below. Young Bradshaw stood quite still. In his heart was much fear - fear of laughter, of ridicule, of failure. But of no other kind of fear. Softly, silently he turned his bicycle so that it faced down the long hill he had just climbed. Then he snapped off the light. He had been reliably informed that in ambush at every fifty yards along the road to Blakeney, sentries were waiting to fire on him. And he proposed to run the gauntlet. He saw that it was for this moment that, first as a volunteer and later as a Territorial, he had drilled in the town hall, practiced on the rifle range, and in mixed manoeuvres slept in six inches of mud. As he threw his leg across his bicycle, Herbert, from the motor-car farther up the hill, fired two shots over his head. These, he explained to Ford, were intended to give " verisimilitude to an otherwise bald and unconvincing narrative." And the sighing of the bullets gave young Bradshaw exactly what he wanted - the assurance that he was not the victim of a practical joke. He threw his weight forward and, lifting his feet, coasted downhill at forty miles an hour into the main street of Blakeney. Ten minutes later, when the car followed, a mob of men so completely blocked the water-front that Ford was forced to stop. His head-lights illuminated hundreds of faces, anxious, sceptical, eager. A gentleman with a white mustache and a look of a retired army officer pushed his way toward Ford, the crowd making room for him, and then closing in his wake.

"Have you seen any - any soldiers?" he demanded.

"German soldiers!" Ford answered. "They tried to catch us, but when I saw who they were, I ran through them to warn you. They fired and - "

"How many - and where?"

"A half-company at Stiffkey and a half-mile farther on a regiment. We didn't know then they were Germans, not until they stopped us. You'd better telephone the garrison, and - "

"Thank you!" snapped the elderly gentleman. "I happen to be in command of this district. What are your names?"

Ford pushed the car forward, parting the crowd.

"I've no time for that!" he called. "We've got to warn every coast town in Norfolk. You take my tip and get London on the long distance!"

As they ran through the night Ford spoke over his shoulder.

"We've got them guessing," he said. "Now, what we want is a live wire, some one with imagination, some one with authority who will wake the countryside."

"Looks ahead there," said Birrell, "as though it hadn't gone to bed."

Before them, as on a Mafeking night, every window in Cley shone with lights. In the main street were fishermen, shopkeepers, "trippers" in flannels, summer residents. The women had turned out as though to witness a display of fireworks. Girls were clinging to the arms of their escorts, shivering in delighted terror. The proprietor of the Red Lion sprang in front of the car and waved his arms.

"What's this tale about Germans?" he demanded jocularly.

"You can see their lights from the beach," said Ford. "They've landed two regiments between here and Wells. Stiffkey is taken, and they've cut all the wires south."

The proprietor refused to be "had."

"Let 'em all come!" he mocked.

" All right, " returned Ford. "Let 'em come, but don't

take it lying down! Get those women off the streets, and go down to the beach, and drive the Germans back! Gangway," he shouted, and the car shot forward. "We warned you," he called, "And it's up to you to - "

His words were lost in the distance. But behind him a man's voice rose with a roar like a rocket and was met with a savage, deep-throated cheer.

Outside the village Ford brought the car to a halt and swung in his seat.

"This thing is going to fail!" he cried petulantly. "They don't believe us. We've got to show ourselves - many times - in a dozen places."

"The British mind moves slowly," said Birrell, the Irishman. "Now, if this had happened in my native land - "

He was interrupted by the screech of a siren, and a demon car that spurned the road, that splattered them with pebbles, tore past and disappeared in the darkness. As it fled down the lane of their head-lights, they saw that men in khaki clung to its sides, were packed in its tonneau, were swaying from its running boards. Before they could find their voices a motor cycle, driven as though the angel of death were at the wheel, shaved their mud-guard and, in its turn, vanished into the night.

"Things are looking up!" said Ford. "Where is our next stop? As I said before, what we want is a live one."

Herbert pressed his electric torch against his road map.

"We are next billed to appear," he said, "about a quarter of a mile from here, at the signal-tower of the Great Eastern Railroad, where we visit the night telegraph operator and give him the surprise party of his life."

The three men had mounted the steps of the signal-tower so quietly that, when the operator heard them, they already surrounded him. He saw three German soldiers with fierce upturned mustaches, with flat, squat helmets, with long brown rifles. They saw an anæmic, pale-faced youth without a coat or collar, for the night was warm, who sank back limply in his chair and gazed speechless with wide-bulging eyes.

In harsh, guttural tones Ford addressed him. "You are a prisoner," he said. "We take over this office in the name of the German Emperor. Get out!"

As though instinctively seeking his only weapon of defence, the hand of the boy operator moved across the table to the key of his instrument. Ford flung his rifle upon it.

"No, you don't!" he growled. "Get out!"

With eyes still bulging, the boy lifted himself into a sitting posture.

"My pay - my month's pay?" he stammered. "Can I take It?"

The expression on the face of the conqueror relaxed.

"Take it and get out," Ford commanded.

With eyes still fixed in fascinated terror upon the invader, the boy pulled open the drawer of the table before him and fumbled with the papers inside.

"Quick!" cried Ford.

The boy was very quick. His hand leaped from the drawer like a snake, and Ford found himself looking into a revolver of the largest calibre issued by a civilized people. Birrell fell upon the boy's shoulders, Herbert twisted the gun from his fingers and hurled it through the window, and almost as quickly hurled himself down the steps of the tower. Birrell leaped after him. Ford remained only long enough to shout: "Don't touch that instrument! If you attempt to send a message through, we will shoot. We go to cut the wires!"

For a minute, the boy in the tower sat rigid, his ears strained, his heart beating in sharp, suffocating stabs. Then, with his left arm raised to guard his face, he sank to his knees and, leaning forward across the table, inviting as he believed his death, he opened the circuit and through the night flashed out a warning to his people.

When they had taken their places in the car, Herbert touched Ford on the shoulder.

"Your last remark," he said, " was that what we wanted was a live one."

"Don't mention it!" said Ford. "He jammed that gun half down my throat. I can taste it still. Where do we go from here?"

"According to the route we mapped out this afternoon," said Herbert, "We are now scheduled to give exhibitions at the coast towns of Salthouse and Weybourne, but - "

"Not with me!" exclaimed Birrell fiercely. "Those towns have been tipped off by now by Blakeney and Cley, and the Boy Scouts would club us to death. I vote we take the back roads to Morston, and drop in on a lonely Coast Guard. If a Coast Guard sees us, the authorities will have to believe him, and they'll call out the navy."

Herbert consulted his map.

"There is a Coast Guard," he said, "stationed just the other side of Morston. And," he added fervently, "let us hope he's lonely."

They lost their way in the back roads, and when they again reached the coast an hour had passed. It was now quite dark. There were no stars, nor moon, but after they had left the car in a side lane and had stepped out upon the cliff, they saw for miles along the coast great beacon fires burning fiercely.

Herbert came to an abrupt halt.

"Since seeing those fires," he explained, "I feel a strange reluctance about showing myself in this uniform to a Coast Guard."

"Coast Guards don't shoot!" mocked Birrell. "They only look at the clouds through a telescope. Three Germans with rifles ought to be able to frighten one Coast Guard with a telescope."

The whitewashed cabin of the Coast Guard was perched on the edge of the cliff. Behind it the downs ran back to meet the road. The door of the cabin was open and from it a shaft of light cut across a tiny garden and showed the white fence and the walk of shells.

"We must pass in single file in front of that light," whispered Ford, "And then, after we are sure he has seen us, we must run like the devil!"

"I'm on in that last scene," growled Herbert.

"Only," repeated Ford with emphasis, "We must be sure he has seen us."

Not twenty feet from them came a bursting roar, a flash, many roars, many flashes, many bullets.

"He's seen us!" yelled Birrell.

After the light from his open door had shown him one German soldier fully armed, the Coast Guard had seen nothing further. But judging from the shrieks of terror and the sounds of falling bodies that followed his first shot, he was convinced he was hemmed in by an army, and he proceeded to sell his life dearly. Clip after clip of cartridges he emptied into the night, now to the front, now to the rear, now out to sea, now at his own shadow in the lamp-light. To the people a quarter of a mile away at Morston it sounded like a battle.

After running half a mile, Ford, bruised and breathless, fell at full length on the grass beside the car. Near it, tearing from his person the last vestiges of a German uniform, he found Birrell. He also was puffing painfully.

"What happened to Herbert?" panted Ford.

"I don't know," gasped Birrell, "When I saw him last he was diving over the cliff into the sea. How many times did you die?"

"About twenty!" groaned the American, "And, besides being dead, I am severely wounded. Every time he fired, I fell on my face, and each time I hit a rock!"

A scarecrow of a figure appeared suddenly in the rays of the head-lights. It was Herbert, scratched, bleeding, dripping with water, and clad simply in a shirt and trousers. He dragged out his kit bag and fell into his golf clothes.

"Anybody who wants a perfectly good German uniform," he cried, "can have mine. I left it in the first row of breakers. It didn't fit me, anyway."

The other two uniforms were hidden in the seat of the car. The rifles and helmets, to lend color to the invasion, were dropped in the open road, and five minutes later three gentlemen in inconspicuous Harris tweeds, and with golf clubs protruding from every part of their car, turned into the shore road to Cromer. What they saw brought swift terror to their guilty souls and the car to an abrupt halt. Before them was a regiment of regulars advancing in column of fours, at the " double." An officer sprang to the front of the car and seated himself beside Ford.

"I'll have to commandeer this," he said. "Run back to Cromer. Don't crush my men, but go like the devil!"

"We heard firing here," explained the officer " at the Coast Guard station. The Guard drove them back to the sea. He counted over a dozen. They made pretty poor practice, for he isn't wounded, but his gravel walk looks as though some one had drawn a harrow over it. I wonder," exclaimed the officer suddenly, "if you are the three gentlemen who first gave the alarm to Colonel Raglan and then went on to warn the other coast towns. Because, if you are, he wants your names."

Ford considered rapidly. If he gave false names and that fact were discovered, they would be suspected and investigated, and the worst might happen. So he replied that his friends and himself probably were the men to whom the officer referred. He explained they had been returning from Cromer, where they had gone to play golf, when they had been held up by the Germans.

"You were lucky to escape," said the officer "And in keeping on to give warning you were taking chances. If I may say so, we think you behaved extremely well."

Ford could not answer. His guilty conscience shamed him into silence. With his siren shrieking and his horn tooting, he was forcing the car through lanes of armed men. They packed each side of the road. They were banked behind the hedges. Their camp-fires blazed from every hill-top.

"Your regiment seems to have turned out to a man!" exclaimed Ford admiringly.

"MY regiment!" snorted the officer. "You've passed through five regiments already, and there are as many more in the dark places. They're everywhere!" he cried jubilantly.

"And I thought they were only where you see the camp-fires," exclaimed Ford.

"That's what the Germans think," said the officer. "It's working like a clock," he cried happily. "There hasn't been a hitch. As soon as they got your warning to Colonel Raglan, they came down to the coast like a wave, on foot, by trains, by motors, and at nine o'clock the Government took over all the railroads. The county regiments, regulars, yeomanry, territorials, have been spread along this shore for thirty miles. Down in London the Guards started to Dover and Brighton two hours ago. The Automobile Club in the first hour collected two hundred cars and turned them over to the Guards in Bird Cage Walk. Cody and Grahame-White and eight of his air men left Hendon an hour ago to reconnoitre the south coast. Admiral Beatty has started with the Channel Squadron to head off the German convoy in the North Sea, and the torpedo destroyers have been sent to lie outside of Heligoland. We'll get that back by daylight. And on land every one of the three services is under arms. On this coast alone before sunrise we'll have one hundred thousand men, and from Colchester the brigade division of artillery, from Ipswich the R. H. A.'s with siege-guns, field-guns, quick-firing-guns, all kinds of guns spread out over every foot of ground from here to Hunstanton. They thought they'd give us a surprise party. They will never give us another surprise party!"

On the top of the hill at Overstrand, the headwaiter of the East Cliff Hotel and the bearded German stood in the garden back of the house with the forbidding walls.

From the road in front came unceasingly the tramp and shuffle of thousands of marching feet, the rumble of heavy cannon, the clanking of their chains, the voices of men trained to command raised in sharp, confident orders. The sky was illuminated by countless fires. Every window of every cottage and hotel blazed with lights. The night had been turned into day. The eyes of the two Germans were like the eyes of those who had passed through an earthquake, of those who looked upon the burning of San Francisco, upon the destruction of Messina.

"We were betrayed, general," whispered the head-waiter.

"We were betrayed, baron," replied the bearded one.

"But you were in time to warn the flotilla."

With a sigh, the older man nodded.

"The last message I received over the wireless," he said, "before I destroyed it, read, 'Your message understood. We are returning. Our movements will be explained as manoeuvres. And," added the general, "The English, having driven us back, will be willing to officially accept that explanation. As manoeuvres, this night will go down into history. Return to the hotel," he commanded, "And in two months you can rejoin your regiment."

On the morning after the invasion the New York Republic published a map of Great Britain that covered three columns and a wood-cut of Ford that was spread over five. Beneath it was printed: "Lester Ford, our London correspondent, captured by the Germans; he escapes and is the first to warn the English people."

On the same morning, In an editorial in The Times of London, appeared this paragraph:

"The Germans were first seen by the Hon. Arthur Herbert, the eldest son of Lord Cinaris; Mr. Patrick Headford Birrell - both of Balliol College, Oxford; and Mr. Lester Ford, the correspondent of the New York Republic. These gentlemen escaped from the landing party that tried to make them prisoners, and at great risk proceeded in their motor-car over roads infested by the Germans to all the coast towns of Norfolk, warning the authorities. Should the war office fail to recognize their services, the people of Great Britain will prove that they are not ungrateful."

A week later three young men sat at dinner on the terrace of the Savoy.

"Shall we, or shall we not," asked Herbert, "tell my uncle that we three, and we three alone, were the invaders?"

"That's hardly correct," said Ford, "as we now know there were two hundred thousand invaders. We were the only three who got ashore."

"I vote we don't tell him," said Birrell. "Let him think with everybody else that the Germans blundered; that an advance party landed too soon and gave the show away. If we talk," he argued, "We'll get credit for a successful hoax. If we keep quiet, everybody will continue to think we saved England. I'm content to let it go at that."

Chapter 4.

BLOOD WILL TELL

David Greene was an employee of the Burdett Automatic Punch Company. The manufacturing plant of the company was at Bridgeport, but in the New York offices there were working samples of all the punches, from the little nickel-plated hand punch with which conductors squeezed holes in railroad tickets, to the big punch that could bite into an iron plate as easily as into a piece of pie. David's duty was to explain these different punches, and accordingly when Burdett Senior or one of the sons turned a customer over to David he spoke of him as a salesman. But David called himself a "demonstrator." For a short time he even succeeded in persuading the other salesmen to speak of themselves as demonstrators, but the shipping clerks and bookkeepers laughed them out of it. They could not laugh David out of it. This was so, partly because he had no sense of humor, and partly because he had a great-great-grandfather. Among the salesmen on lower Broadway, to possess a great-great-grandfather is unusual, even a great-grandfather is a rarity, and either is considered superfluous. But to David the possession of a great-great-grandfather was a precious and open delight. He had possessed him only for a short time. Undoubtedly he always had existed, but it was not until David's sister Anne married a doctor in

Bordentown, New Jersey, and became socially ambitious, that David emerged as a Son of Washington.

It was sister Anne, anxious to "get in" as a "Daughter" and wear a distaff pin in her shirtwaist, who discovered the revolutionary ancestor. She unearthed him, or rather ran him to earth, in the graveyard of the Presbyterian church at Bordentown. He was no less a person than General Hiram Greene, and he had fought with Washington at Trenton and at Princeton. Of this there was no doubt. That, later, on moving to New York, his descendants became peace-loving salesmen did not affect his record. To enter a society founded on heredity, the important thing is first to catch your ancestor, and having made sure of him, David entered the Society of the Sons of Washington with flying colors. He was not unlike the man who had been speaking prose for forty years without knowing it. He was not unlike the other man who woke to find himself famous. He had gone to bed a timid, near-sighted, underpaid salesman without a relative in the world, except a married sister in Bordentown, and he awoke to find he was a direct descendant of "Neck or Nothing" Greene, a revolutionary hero, a friend of Washington, a man whose portrait hung in the State House at Trenton. David's life had lacked color. The day he carried his certificate of membership to the big jewelry store uptown and purchased two rosettes, one for each of his two coats, was the proudest of his life.

The other men in the Broadway office took a different view. As Wyckoff, one of Burdett's flying squadron of travelling salesmen, said, "All grandfathers look alike to me, whether they're great, or great-great-great. Each one is as dead as the other. I'd rather have a live cousin who could loan me a five, or slip me a drink. What did your great-great dad ever do for you?"

"Well, for one thing," said David stiffly, "he fought in the War of the Revolution. He saved us from the shackles of monarchical England; he made it possible for me and you to enjoy the liberties of a free republic."

"Don't try to tell me your grandfather did all that," protested Wyckoff, "because I know better. There were a lot of others helped. I read about it in a book."

"I am not grudging glory to others," returned David; "I am only saying I am proud that I am a descendant of a revolutionist."

Wyckoff dived into his inner pocket and produced a leather photograph frame that folded like a concertina.

"I don't want to be a descendant," he said; "I'd rather be an ancestor. Look at those." Proudly he exhibited photographs of Mrs. Wyckoff with the baby and of three other little Wyckoffs. David looked with envy at the children.

"When I'm married," he stammered, and at the words he blushed, "I hope to be an ancestor."

"If you're thinking of getting married," said Wyckoff, "you'd better hope for a raise in salary."

The other clerks were as unsympathetic as Wyckoff. At first when David showed them his parchment certificate, and his silver gilt insignia with on one side a portrait of Washington, and on the other a

Continental soldier, they admitted it was dead swell. They even envied him, not the grandfather, but the fact that owing to that distinguished relative David was constantly receiving beautifully engraved invitations to attend the monthly meetings of the society; to subscribe to a fund to erect monuments on battle-fields to mark neglected graves; to join in joyous excursions to the tomb of Washington or of John Paul Jones; to inspect West Point, Annapolis, and Bunker Hill; to be among those present at the annual "banquet" at Delmonico's. In order that when he opened these letters he might have an audience, he had given the society his office address.

In these communications he was always addressed as "Dear Compatriot," and never did the words fail to give him a thrill. They seemed to lift him out of Burdett's salesrooms and Broadway, and place him next to things uncommercial, untainted, high, and noble. He did not quite know what an aristocrat was, but he believed being a compatriot made him an aristocrat. When customers were rude, when Mr. John or Mr. Robert was overbearing, this idea enabled David to rise above their ill-temper, and he would smile and say to himself: "If they knew the meaning of the blue rosette in my button-hole, how differently they would treat me! How easily with a word could I crush them!"

But few of the customers recognized the significance of the button. They thought it meant that David belonged to the Y. M. C. A. or was a teetotaler. David, with his gentle manners and pale, ascetic face, was liable to give that impression.

When Wyckoff mentioned marriage, the reason David

blushed was because, although no one in the office suspected it, he wished to marry the person in whom the office took the greatest pride. This was Miss Emily Anthony, one of Burdett and Sons' youngest, most efficient, and prettiest stenographers, and although David did not cut as dashing a figure as did some of the firm's travelling men, Miss Anthony had found something in him so greatly to admire that she had, out of office hours, accepted his devotion, his theatre tickets, and an engagement ring. Indeed, so far had matters progressed, that it had been almost decided when in a few months they would go upon their vacations they also would go upon their honeymoon. And then a cloud had come between them, and from a quarter from which David had expected only sunshine.

The trouble befell when David discovered he had a great-great-grandfather. With that fact itself Miss Anthony was almost as pleased as was David himself, but while he was content to bask in another's glory, Miss Anthony saw in his inheritance only an incentive to achieve glory for himself.

From a hard-working salesman she had asked but little, but from a descendant of a national hero she expected other things. She was a determined young person, and for David she was an ambitious young person. She found she was dissatisfied. She found she was disappointed. The great-great-grandfather had opened up a new horizon - had, in a way, raised the standard. She was as fond of David as always, but his tales of past wars and battles, his accounts of present banquets at which he sat shoulder to shoulder with men of whom even Burdett and Sons spoke with awe, touched her imagination.

"You shouldn't be content to just wear a button," she urged. "If you're a Son of Washington, you ought to act like one."

"I know I'm not worthy of you," David sighed.

"I don't mean that, and you know I don't," Emily replied indignantly. "It has nothing to do with me! I want you to be worthy of yourself, of your grandpa Hiram!"

"But HOW?" complained David. "What chance has a twenty-five dollar a week clerk - "

It was a year before the Spanish-American War, while the patriots of Cuba were fighting the mother country for their independence.

"If I were a Son of the Revolution," said Emily, "I'd go to Cuba and help free it."

"Don't talk nonsense," cried David. "If I did that I'd lose my job, and we'd never be able to marry. Besides, what's Cuba done for me? All I know about Cuba is, I once smoked a Cuban cigar and it made me ill."

"Did Lafayette talk like that?" demanded Emily. "Did he ask what have the American rebels ever done for me?"

"If I were in Lafayette's class," sighed David, "I wouldn't be selling automatic punches."

"There's your trouble," declared Emily "You lack self-confidence. You're too humble, you've got fighting blood and you ought to keep saying to yourself, 'Blood will tell,' and the first thing you know, it WILL tell! You might begin by going into politics in your ward. Or, you could join the militia. That takes only one night a week, and then, if we DID go to war with Spain, you'd get a commission, and come back a captain!"

Emily's eyes were beautiful with delight. But the sight gave David no pleasure. In genuine distress, he shook his head.

"Emily," he said, "you're going to be awfully disappointed in me."

Emily's eyes closed as though they shied at some mental picture. But when she opened them they were bright, and her smile was kind and eager.

"No, I'm not," she protested; "only I want a husband with a career, and one who'll tell me to keep quiet when I try to run it for him."

"I've often wished you would," said David.

"Would what? Run your career for you?"

"No, keep quiet. Only it didn't seem polite to tell you so."

"Maybe I'd like you better," said Emily, "if you weren't so darned polite."

A week later, early in the spring of 1897, the unexpected happened, and David was promoted into the flying squadron. He now was a travelling salesman, with a rise in salary and a commission on orders. It was a step forward, but as going on the road meant absence from Emily, David was not elated. Nor did it satisfy Emily. It was not money she wanted. Her ambition for David could not be silenced with a raise in wages. She did not say this, but David knew that in him she still found something lacking, and when they said good-by they both were ill at ease and completely unhappy. Formerly, each day when Emily in passing David in the office said good-morning, she used to add the number of the days that still separated them from the vacation which also was to be their honeymoon. But, for the last month she had stopped counting the days - at least she did not count them aloud.

David did not ask her why this was so. He did not dare. And, sooner than learn the truth that she had decided not to marry him, or that she was even considering not marrying him, he asked no questions, but in ignorance of her present feelings set forth on his travels. Absence from Emily hurt just as much as he had feared it would. He missed her, needed her, longed for her. In numerous letters he told her so. But, owing to the frequency with which he moved, her letters never caught up with him. It was almost a relief. He did not care to think of what they might tell him.

The route assigned David took him through the South and kept him close to the Atlantic seaboard. In obtaining orders he was not unsuccessful, and at the end of the first month received from the firm a telegram of congratulation. This was of importance chiefly because it might please Emily. But he knew that in her eyes the great-great-grandson of Hiram Greene could not rest content with a telegram from Burdett and Sons. A year before she would have considered it a high honor, a cause for celebration.

Now, he could see her press her pretty lips together and shake her pretty head. It was not enough. But how could he accomplish more. He began to hate his great-great-grandfather. He began to wish Hiram Greene had lived and died a bachelor.

And then Dame Fortune took David in hand and toyed with him and spanked him, and pelted and petted him, until finally she made him her favorite son. Dame Fortune went about this work in an abrupt and arbitrary manner.

On the night of the 1st of March, 1897, two trains were scheduled to leave the Union Station at Jacksonville at exactly the same minute, and they left exactly on time. As never before in the history of any Southern railroad has this miracle occurred, it shows that when Dame Fortune gets on the job she is omnipotent. She placed David on the train to Miami as the train he wanted drew out for Tampa, and an hour later, when the conductor looked at David's ticket, he pulled the bell-cord and dumped David over the side into the heart of a pine forest. If he walked back along the track for one mile, the conductor reassured him, he would find a flag station where at midnight he could flag a train going north. In an hour it would deliver him safely in Jacksonville.

There was a moon, but for the greater part of the time it was hidden by fitful, hurrying clouds, and, as David stumbled forward, at one moment he would see the rails like streaks of silver, and the next would be encompassed in a complete and bewildering darkness. He made his way from tie to tie only by feeling with his foot. After an hour he came to a shed. Whether it was or was not the flag station the conductor had in mind, he did not know, and he never did know. He was too tired, too hot, and too disgusted to proceed, and dropping his suit case he sat down under the open roof of the shed prepared to wait either for the train or daylight. So far as he could see, on every side of him stretched a swamp, silent, dismal, interminable. From its black water rose dead trees, naked of bark and hung with streamers of funereal moss. There was not a sound or sign of human habitation. The silence was the silence of the ocean at night David remembered the berth reserved for him on the train to Tampa and of the loathing with which he had considered placing himself between its sheets. But now how gladly would he welcome it! For, in the sleeping-car, ill-smelling, close, and stuffy, he at least would have been surrounded by fellow-sufferers of his own species. Here his companions were owls, water-snakes, and sleeping buzzards.

I am alone," he told himself, "on a railroad embankment, entirely surrounded by alligators."

And then he found he was not alone.

In the darkness, illuminated by a match, not a hundred yards from him there flashed suddenly the face of a man. Then the match went out and the face with it. David noted that it had appeared at some height above the level of the swamp, at an elevation higher even than that of the embankment. It was as though the man had been sitting on the limb of a tree. David crossed the tracks and found that on the side of the embankment opposite the shed there was solid ground and what once had been a wharf. He advanced over this cautiously, and as he did so the clouds disappeared, and in the full light of the moon he saw a bayou broadening into a river, and made fast to the decayed and rotting wharf an ocean-going tug. It was from her deck that the man, in lighting his pipe, had shown his face. At the thought of a warm engine-room and the company of his fellow creatures, David's heart leaped with pleasure. He advanced quickly. And then something in the appearance of the tug, something mysterious, secretive, threatening, caused him to halt. No lights showed from her engine-room, cabin, or pilot-house. Her decks were empty. But, as was evidenced by the black smoke that rose from her funnel, she was awake and awake to some purpose. David stood uncertainly, questioning whether to make his presence known or return to the loneliness of the shed. The question was decided for him. He had not considered that standing in the moonlight he was a conspicuous figure. The planks of the wharf creaked and a man came toward him. As one who means to attack, or who fears attack, he approached warily. He wore high boots, riding breeches, and a sombrero. He was a little man, but his movements were alert and active. To David he seemed unnecessarily excited. He thrust himself close against David.

"Who the devil are you?" demanded the man from the tug. "How'd you get here?"

"I walked," said David.

"Walked?" the man snorted incredulously.

"I took the wrong train," explained David pleasantly. "They put me off about a mile below here. I walked back to this flag station. I'm going to wait here for the next train north."

The little man laughed mockingly.

"Oh, no you're not," he said. "If you walked here, you can just walk away again!" With a sweep of his arm, he made a vigorous and peremptory gesture.

"You walk!" he commanded.

"I'll do just as I please about that," said David.

As though to bring assistance, the little man started hastily toward the tug.

"I'll find some one who'll make you walk!" he called. "You WAIT, that's all, you WAIT!"

David decided not to wait. It was possible the wharf was private property and he had been trespassing. In any case, at the flag station the rights of all men were equal, and if he were in for a fight he judged it best to choose his own battle-ground. He recrossed the tracks and sat down on his suit case in a dark corner of the shed. Himself hidden in the shadows he could see in the moonlight the approach of any other person.

"They're river pirates," said David to himself, "or smugglers. They're certainly up to some mischief, or why should they object to the presence of a perfectly harmless stranger?"

Partly with cold, partly with nervousness, David shivered.

"I wish that train would come," he sighed. And instantly? As though in answer to his wish, from only a short distance down the track he heard the rumble and creak of approaching cars. In a flash David planned his course of action.

The thought of spending the night in a swamp infested by alligators and smugglers had become intolerable. He must escape, and he must escape by the train now approaching. To that end the train must be stopped. His plan was simple. The train was moving very, very slowly, and though he had no lantern to wave, in order to bring it to a halt he need only stand on the track exposed to the glare of the headlight and wave his arms. David sprang between the rails and gesticulated wildly. But in amazement his arms fell to his sides. For the train, now only a hundred yards distant and creeping toward him at a snail's pace, carried no head-light, and though in the moonlight David was plainly visible, it blew no whistle, tolled no bell. Even the passenger coaches in the rear of the sightless engine were wrapped in darkness. It was a ghost of a train, a Flying Dutchman of a train, a nightmare of a train. It was as unreal as the black swamp, as the moss on the dead trees, as the ghostly tug-boat tied to the rotting wharf.

"Is the place haunted!" exclaimed David.

He was answered by the grinding of brakes and by the train coming to a sharp halt. And instantly from every side men fell from it to the ground, and the silence of the night was broken by a confusion of calls and eager greeting and questions and sharp words of command.

So fascinated was David in the stealthy arrival of the train and in her mysterious passengers that, until they confronted him, he did not note the equally stealthy approach of three men. Of these one was the little man from the tug. With him was a fat, red-faced Irish-American He wore no coat and his shirt-sleeves were drawn away from his hands by garters of pink elastic, his derby hat was balanced behind his ears, upon his right hand flashed an enormous diamond. He looked as though but at that moment he had stopped sliding glasses across a Bowery bar. The third man carried the outward marks of a sailor. David believed he was the tallest man he had ever beheld, but equally remarkable with his height was his beard and hair, which were of a fierce brick-dust red. Even in the mild moonlight it flamed like a torch.

"What's your business?" demanded the man with the flamboyant hair.

"I came here," began David, "to wait for a train - "

The tall man bellowed with indignant rage.

"Yes," he shouted; "this is the sort of place any one would pick out to wait for a train!"

In front of David's nose he shook a fist as large as a catcher's glove. "Don't you lie to ME!" he bullied. "Do you know who I am? Do you know WHO you're up against? I'm - "

The barkeeper person interrupted.

"Never mind who you are," he said. "We know that. Find out who HE is."

David turned appealingly to the barkeeper.

" Do you suppose I'd come here on purpose ? " he

protested. "I'm a travelling man - "

"You won't travel any to-night," mocked the red-haired one. "You've seen what you came to see, and all you want now is to get to a Western Union wire. Well, you don't do it. You don't leave here to-night!"

As though he thought he had been neglected, the little man in riding-boots pushed forward importantly.

"Tie him to a tree!" he suggested.

"Better take him on board," said the barkeeper, "and send him back by the pilot. When we're once at sea, he can't hurt us any."

"What makes you think I want to hurt you?" demanded David. "Who do you think I am?"

"We know who you are," shouted the fiery-headed one. "You're a blanketty-blank spy! You're a government spy or a Spanish spy, and whichever you are you don't get away to-night!"

David had not the faintest idea what the man meant, but he knew his self-respect was being ill-treated, and his self-respect rebelled.

"You have made a very serious mistake," he said, "and whether you like it or not, I AM leaving here to-night, and YOU can go to the devil!"

Turning his back David started with great dignity to walk away. It was a short walk. Something hit him below the ear and he found himself curling up comfortably on the ties. He had a strong desire to sleep, but was conscious that a bed on a railroad track, on account of trains wanting to pass, was unsafe. This doubt did not long disturb him. His head rolled against the steel rail, his limbs relaxed. From a great distance, and in a strange sing-song he heard the voice of the barkeeper saying, "Nine - ten - and OUT!"

When David came to his senses his head was resting on a coil of rope. In his ears was the steady throb of an engine, and in his eyes the glare of a lantern. The lantern was held by a pleasant-faced youth in a golf cap who was smiling sympathetically. David rose on his elbow and gazed wildly about him. He was in the bow of the ocean-going tug, and he saw that from where he lay in the bow to her stern her decks were packed with men. She was steaming swiftly down a broad river. On either side the gray light that comes before the dawn showed low banks studded with stunted palmettos. Close ahead David heard the roar of the surf.

"Sorry to disturb you," said the youth in the golf cap, "but we drop the pilot in a few minutes and you're going with him."

David moved his aching head gingerly, and was conscious of a bump as large as a tennis ball behind his right ear.

"What happened to me?" he demanded.

"You were sort of kidnapped, I guess," laughed the young man. "It was a raw deal, but they couldn't take any chances. The pilot will land you at Okra Point. You can hire a rig there to take you to the railroad."

"But why?" demanded David indignantly. "Why was I kidnapped? What had I done? Who were those men who - "

From the pilot-house there was a sharp jangle of bells to the engine-room, and the speed of the tug slackened.

"Come on," commanded the young man briskly. "The pilot's going ashore. Here's your grip, here's your hat. The ladder's on the port side. Look where you're stepping. We can't show any lights, and it's dark as - "

But, even as he spoke, like a flash of powder, as swiftly as one throws an electric switch, as blindingly as a train leaps from the tunnel into the glaring sun, the darkness vanished and the tug was swept by the fierce, blatant radiance of a search-light.

It was met by shrieks from two hundred throats, by screams, oaths, prayers, by the sharp jangling of bells, by the blind rush of many men scurrying like rats for a hole to hide in, by the ringing orders of one man. Above the tumult this one voice rose like the warning strokes of a fire-gong, and looking up to the pilot-house from whence the voice came, David saw the barkeeper still in his shirt-sleeves and with his derby hat pushed back behind his ears, with one hand clutching the telegraph to the engine-room, with the other holding the spoke of the wheel.

David felt the tug, like a hunter taking a fence, rise in a great leap. Her bow sank and rose, tossing the water from her in black, oily waves, the smoke poured from her funnel, from below her engines sobbed and quivered, and like a hound freed from a leash she raced for the open sea. But swiftly as she fled, as a thief is held in the circle of a policeman's bull's-eye, the shaft of light followed and exposed her and held her in its grip. The youth in the golf cap was clutching David by the arm. With his free hand he pointed down the shaft of light. So great was the tumult that to be heard he brought his lips close to David's ear.

"That's the revenue cutter!" he shouted. "She's been laying for us for three weeks, and now," he shrieked exultingly, "the old man's going to give her a race for it."

From excitement, from cold, from alarm, David's nerves were getting beyond his control.

"But how," he demanded, "how do I get ashore?"

"You don't!"

"When he drops the pilot, don't I - "

"How can he drop the pilot?" yelled the youth. "The pilot's got to stick by the boat. So have you."

David clutched the young man and swung him so that they stood face to face.

"Stick by what boat?" yelled David. "Who are these men? Who are you? What boat is this?"

In the glare of the search-light David saw the eyes of the youth staring at him as though he feared he were in the clutch of a madman. Wrenching himself free, the youth pointed at the pilot-house. Above it on a blue board in letters of gold-leaf a foot high was the name of the tug. As David read it his breath left him, a finger of ice passed slowly down his spine. The name he read was The Three Friends.

"THE THREE FRIENDS!" shrieked David. "She's a filibuster! She's a pirate! Where're we going?

"To Cuba!"

David emitted a howl of anguish, rage, and protest.

"What for?" he shrieked.

The young man regarded him coldly.

"To pick bananas," he said.

"I won't go to Cuba," shouted David. "I've got to work! I'm paid to sell machinery. I demand to be put ashore. I'll lose my job if I'm not put ashore. I'll sue you! I'll have the law - "

David found himself suddenly upon his knees. His first thought was that the ship had struck a rock, and then that she was bumping herself over a succession of coral reefs. She dipped, dived, reared, and plunged. Like a hooked fish, she flung herself in the air, quivering from bow to stern. No longer was David of a mind to sue the filibusters if they did not put him ashore. If only they had put him ashore, in gratitude he would have crawled on his knees. What followed was of no interest to David, nor to many of the filibusters, nor to any of the Cuban patriots. Their groans of self-pity, their prayers and curses in eloquent Spanish, rose high above the crash of broken crockery and the pounding of the waves. Even when the search-light gave way to a brilliant sunlight the circumstance was unobserved by David. Nor was he concerned in the tidings brought forward by the youth in the golf cap, who raced the slippery decks and vaulted the prostrate forms as sure-footedly as a hurdler on a cinder track. To David, in whom he seemed to think he had found a congenial spirit, he shouted Joyfully, "She's fired two blanks at us!" he cried; "now she's firing cannon-balls!"

"Thank God," whispered David; "perhaps she'll sink us!"

But The Three Friends showed her heels to the revenue cutter, and so far as David knew hours passed into days and days into weeks. It was like those nightmares in which in a minute one is whirled through centuries of fear and torment. Sometimes, regardless of nausea, of his aching head, of the hard deck, of the waves that splashed and smothered him, David fell into broken slumber. Sometimes he woke to a dull consciousness of his position. At such moments he added to his misery by speculating upon the other misfortunes that might have befallen him on shore. Emily, he decided, had given him up for lost and married - probably a navy officer in command of a battle-ship. Burdett and Sons had cast him off forever. Possibly his disappearance had caused them to suspect him; even now they might be regarding him as a defaulter, as a fugitive from justice. His accounts, no doubt, were being carefully overhauled. In actual time, two days and two nights had passed; to David it seemed many ages.

On the third day he crawled to the stern, where there seemed less motion, and finding a boat's cushion threw it in the lee scupper and fell upon it. From time to time the youth in the golf cap had brought him food and drink, and he now appeared from the cook's galley bearing a bowl of smoking soup.

David considered it a doubtful attention.

But he said, "You're very kind. How did a fellow like you come to mix up with these pirates?"

The youth laughed good-naturedly.

"They're not pirates, they're patriots," he said, "and I'm not mixed up with them. My name is Henry Carr and I'm a guest of Jimmy Doyle, the captain."

"The barkeeper with the derby hat?" said David.

"He's not a barkeeper, he's a teetotaler," Carr corrected, "and he's the greatest filibuster alive. He knows these waters as you know Broadway, and he's the salt of the earth. I did him a favor once; sort of mouse-helping-the-lion idea. Just through dumb luck I found out about this expedition. The government agents in New York found out I'd found out and sent for me to tell. But I didn't, and I didn't write the story either. Doyle heard about that. So, he asked me to come as his guest, and he's promised that after he's landed the expedition and the arms I can write as much about it as I darn please."

"Then you're a reporter?" said David.

"I'm what we call a cub reporter," laughed Carr. "You see, I've always dreamed of being a war correspondent. The men in the office say I dream too much. They're always guying me about it. But, haven't you noticed, it's the ones who dream who find their dreams come true. Now this isn't real war, but it's a near war, and when the real thing breaks loose, I can tell the managing editor I served as a war correspondent in the Cuban-Spanish campaign. And he may give me a real job!"

"And you LIKE this?" groaned David.

"I wouldn't, if I were as sick as you are," said Carr, "but I've a stomach like a Harlem goat." He stooped and lowered his voice. "Now, here are two fake filibusters," he whispered. "The men you read about in the newspapers. If a man's a REAL filibuster, nobody knows it!"

Coming toward them was the tall man who had knocked David out, and the little one who had wanted to tie him to a tree.

"All they ask," whispered Carr, "is money and advertisement. If they knew I was a reporter, they'd eat out of my hand. The tall man calls himself Lighthouse Harry. He once kept a light-house on the Florida coast, and that's as near to the sea as he ever got. The other one is a dare-devil calling himself Colonel Beamish. He says he's an English officer, and a soldier of fortune, and that he's been in eighteen battles. Jimmy says he's never been near enough to a battle to see the red-cross flags on the base hospital. But they've fooled these Cubans. The Junta thinks they're great fighters, and it's sent them down here to work the machine guns. But I'm afraid the only fighting they will do will be in the sporting columns, and not in the ring."

A half dozen sea-sick Cubans were carrying a heavy, oblong box. They dropped it not two yards from where

David lay, and with a screwdriver Lighthouse Harry proceeded to open the lid.

Carr explained to David that The Three Friends was approaching that part of the coast of Cuba on which she had arranged to land her expedition, and that in case she was surprised by one of the Spanish patrol boats she was preparing to defend herself.

"They've got an automatic gun in that crate," said Carr, "and they're going to assemble it. You'd better move; they'll be tramping all over you.

David shook his head feebly.

"I can't move!" he protested. "I wouldn't move if it would free Cuba."

For several hours with very languid interest David watched Lighthouse Harry and Colonel Beamish screw a heavy tripod to the deck and balance above it a quick-firing one-pounder. They worked very slowly, and to David, watching them from the lee scupper, they appeared extremely unintelligent.

"I don't believe either of those thugs put an automatic gun together in his life," he whispered to Carr. "I never did, either, but I've put hundreds of automatic punches together, and I bet that gun won't work."

"What's wrong with it?" said Carr.

Before David could summon sufficient energy to answer, the attention of all on board was diverted, and by a single word.

Whether the word is whispered apologetically by the smoking-room steward to those deep in bridge, or shrieked from the tops of a sinking ship it never quite fails of its effect. A sweating stoker from the engine-room saw it first.

"Land!" he hailed.

The sea-sick Cubans raised themselves and swung their hats; their voices rose in a fierce chorus.

"Cuba libre!" they yelled.

The sun piercing the morning mists had uncovered a coast-line broken with bays and inlets. Above it towered green hills, the peak of each topped by a squat blockhouse; in the valleys and water courses like columns of marble rose the royal palms.

"You MUST look!" Carr entreated David. "it's just as it is in the pictures!

"Then I don't have to look," groaned David.

The Three Friends was making for a point of land that curved like a sickle. On the inside of the sickle was Nipe Bay. On the opposite shore of that broad harbor at the place of rendezvous a little band of Cubans waited to receive the filibusters. The goal was in sight. The dreadful voyage was done. Joy and excitement thrilled the ship's company. Cuban patriots appeared in uniforms with Cuban flags pinned in the brims of their straw sombreros. From the hold came boxes of small-arm ammunition of Mausers, rifles, machetes, and saddles. To protect the landing a box of shells was placed in readiness beside the one-pounder.

"In two hours, if we have smooth water," shouted Lighthouse Harry, "we ought to get all of this on shore. And then, all I ask," he cried mightily, "is for some one to kindly show me a Spaniard!"

His heart's desire was instantly granted. He was shown not only one Spaniard, but several Spaniards. They were on the deck of one of the fastest gun-boats of the Spanish navy. Not a mile from The Three Friends she sprang from the cover of a narrow inlet. She did not signal questions or extend courtesies. For her the name of the ocean-going tug was sufficient introduction. Throwing ahead of her a solid shell, she raced in pursuit, and as The Three Friends leaped to full speed there came from the gun-boat the sharp dry crackle of Mausers.

With an explosion of terrifying oaths Lighthouse Harry thrust a shell into the breech of the quick-firing gun. Without waiting to aim it, he tugged at the trigger. Nothing happened! He threw open the breech and gazed impotently at the base of the shell. It was untouched. The ship was ringing with cries of anger, of hate, with rat-like squeaks of fear.

Above the heads of the filibusters a shell screamed and within a hundred feet splashed into a wave.

From his mat in the lee scupper David groaned miserably. He was far removed from any of the greater emotions.

"It's no use!" he protested. "They can't do! It's not connected!"

" WHAT'S not connected ?" yelled Carr. He fell upon

David. He half-lifted, half-dragged him to his feet.

"If you know what's wrong with that gun, you fix it! Fix it," he shouted, "or I'll - "

David was not concerned with the vengeance Carr threatened. For, on the instant a miracle had taken place. With the swift insidiousness of morphine, peace ran through his veins, soothed his racked body, his jangled nerves. The Three Friends had made the harbor, and was gliding through water flat as a pond. But David did not know why the change had come. He knew only that his soul and body were at rest, that the sun was shining, that he had passed through the valley of the shadow, and once more was a sane, sound young man.

With a savage thrust of the shoulder he sent Lighthouse Harry sprawling from the gun. With swift, practised fingers he fell upon its mechanism. He wrenched it apart. He lifted it, reset, readjusted it.

Ignorant themselves, those about him saw that he understood, saw that his work was good.

They raised a joyous, defiant cheer. But a shower of bullets drove them to cover, bullets that ripped the deck, splintered the superstructure, smashed the glass in the air ports, like angry wasps sang in a continuous whining chorus. Intent only on the gun, David worked feverishly. He swung to the breech, locked it, and dragged it open, pulled on the trigger and found it gave before his forefinger.

He shouted with delight.

"I've got it working," he yelled.

He turned to his audience, but his audience had fled. From beneath one of the life-boats protruded the riding-boots of Colonel Beamish, the tall form of Lighthouse Harry was doubled behind a water butt. A shell splashed to port, a shell splashed to starboard. For an instant David stood staring wide-eyed at the greyhound of a boat that ate up the distance between them, at the jets of smoke and stabs of flame that sprang from her bow, at the figures crouched behind her gunwale, firing in volleys.

To David it came suddenly, convincingly, that in a dream he had lived it all before, and something like raw poison stirred in David, something leaped to his throat and choked him, something rose in his brain and made him see scarlet. He felt rather than saw young Carr kneeling at the box of ammunition, and holding a shell toward him. He heard the click as the breech shut, felt the rubber tire of the brace give against the weight of his shoulder, down a long shining tube saw the pursuing gun-boat , saw her again and many times disappear behind a flash of flame. A bullet gashed his forehead, a bullet passed deftly through his forearm, but he did not heed them. Confused with the thrashing of the engines, with the roar of the gun he heard a strange voice shrieking unceasingly:

"Cuba libre!" it yelled. "To hell with Spain!" and he found that the voice was his own.

The story lost nothing in the way Carr wrote it.

" And the best of it is, " he exclaimed joyfully,

"it's true!"

For a Spanish gun-boat HAD been crippled and forced to run herself aground by a tug-boat manned by Cuban patriots, and by a single gun served by one man, and that man an American. It was the first sea-fight of the war. Over night a Cuban navy had been born, and into the limelight a cub reporter had projected a new "hero," a ready-made, warranted-not-to-run, popular idol.

They were seated in the pilot-house, "Jimmy" Doyle, Carr, and David, the patriots and their arms had been safely dumped upon the coast of Cuba, and The Three Friends was gliding swiftly and, having caught the Florida straits napping, smoothly toward Key West. Carr had just finished reading aloud his account of the engagement.

You will tell the story just as I have written it," commanded the proud author. "Your being South as a travelling salesman was only a blind. You came to volunteer for this expedition. Before you could explain your wish you were mistaken for a secret-service man, and hustled on board. That was just where you wanted to be, and when the moment arrived you took command of the ship and single-handed won the naval battle of Nipe Bay."

Jimmy Doyle nodded his head approvingly. "You certainty did, Dave," protested the great man, "I seen you when you done it!"

At Key West Carr filed his story and while the hospital surgeons kept David there over one steamer, to dress his wounds, his fame and features spread across the map of the United States.

Burdett and Sons basked in reflected glory. Reporters besieged their office. At the Merchants Down-Town Club the business men of lower Broadway tendered congratulations.

"Of course, it's a great surprise to us," Burdett and Sons would protest and wink heavily. "Of course, when the boy asked to be sent South we'd no idea he was planning to fight for Cuba! Or we wouldn't have let him go, would we?" Then again they would wink heavily. "I suppose you know," they would say, "that he's a direct descendant of General Hiram Greene, who won the battle of Trenton. What I say is, 'Blood will tell!'" And then in a body every one in the club would move against the bar and exclaim: "Here's to Cuba libre!"

When the Olivette from Key West reached Tampa Bay every Cuban in the Tampa cigar factories was at the dock. There were thousands of them and all of the Junta, in high hats, to read David an address of welcome.

And, when they saw him at the top of the gang-plank with his head in a bandage and his arm in a sling, like a mob of maniacs they howled and surged toward him. But before they could reach their hero the courteous Junta forced them back, and cleared a pathway for a young girl. She was travel-worn and pale, her shirt-waist was disgracefully wrinkled, her best hat was a wreck. No one on Broadway would have recognized her as Burdett and Sons' most immaculate and beautiful stenographer.

She dug the shapeless hat into David's shoulder, and clung to him. "David!" she sobbed, "promise me you'll never, never do it again!"

Chapter 5.

THE SAILORMAN

Before Latimer put him on watch, the Nantucket sailorman had not a care in the world. If the wind blew from the north, he spun to the left; if it came from the south, he spun to the right. But it was entirely the wind that was responsible. So, whichever way he turned, he smiled broadly, happily. His outlook upon the world was that of one who loved his fellowman. He had many brothers as like him as twins all over Nantucket and Cape Cod and the North Shore, smiling from the railings of verandas, from the roofs of bungalows, from the eaves of summer palaces. Empaled on their little iron uprights, each sailorman whirled - sometimes languidly, like a great lady revolving to the slow measures of a waltz, sometimes so rapidly that he made you quite dizzy, and had he not been a sailorman with a heart of oak and a head and stomach of pine, he would have been quite seasick. But the particular sailorman that Latimer bought for Helen Page and put on sentry duty carried on his shoulders most grave and unusual responsibilities. He was the guardian of a buried treasure, the keeper of the happiness of two young people. It was really asking a great deal of a care-free, happy-go-lucky weather-vane.

Every summer from Boston Helen Page's people had

been coming to Fair Harbor. They knew it when what now is the polo field was their cow pasture. And whether at the age of twelve or of twenty or more, Helen Page ruled Fair Harbor. When she arrived the "season" opened; when she departed the local trades-people sighed and began to take account of stock. She was so popular because she possessed charm, and because she played no favorites. To the grooms who held the ponies on the sidelines her manner was just as simple and interested as it was to the gilded youths who came to win the championship cups and remained to try to win Helen. She was just as genuinely pleased to make a four at tennis with the "kids" as to take tea on the veranda of the club-house with the matrons. To each her manner was always as though she were of their age. When she met the latter on the beach road, she greeted them riotously and joyfully by their maiden names. And the matrons liked it. In comparison the deference shown them by the other young women did not so strongly appeal.

"When I'm jogging along in my station wagon," said one of them, "and Helen shrieks and waves at me from her car, I feel as though I were twenty, and I believe that she is really sorry I am not sitting beside her, instead of that good-looking Latimer man, who never wears a hat. Why does he never wear a hat? Because he knows he's good-looking, or because Helen drives so fast he can't keep it on?"

"Does he wear a hat when he is not with Helen?" asked the new arrival. "That might help some."

"We will never know," exclaimed the young matron; "he never leaves her."

This was so true that it had become a public scandal. You met them so many times a day driving together, motoring together, playing golf together, that you were embarrassed for them and did not know which way to look. But they gloried in their shame. If you tactfully pretended not to see them, Helen shouted at you. She made you feel you had been caught doing something indelicate and underhand.

The mothers of Fair Harbor were rather slow in accepting young Latimer. So many of their sons had seen Helen shake her head in that inarticulate, worried way, and look so sorry for them, that any strange young man who apparently succeeded where those who had been her friends for years had learned they must remain friends, could not hope to escape criticism. Besides, they did not know him: he did not come from Boston and Harvard, but from a Western city. They were told that at home, at both the law and the game of politics, he worked hard and successfully; but it was rather held against him by the youth of Fair Harbor that he played at there games, not so much for the sake of the game as for exercise. He put aside many things, such as whiskey and soda at two in the morning, and bridge all afternoon, with the remark: "I find it does not tend toward efficiency." It was a remark that irritated and, to the minds of the men at the country clubs, seemed to place him. They liked to play polo because they liked to play polo, not because it kept their muscles limber and their brains clear.

"Some Western people were telling me," said one of the matrons, "that he wants to be the next lieutenant-governor. They say he is very ambitious and very selfish."

"Any man is selfish," protested one who for years had attempted to marry Helen, "who wants to keep Helen to himself. But that he should wish to be a lieutenant-governor, too, is rather an anticlimax. It makes one lose sympathy."

Latimer went on his way without asking any sympathy. The companionship of Helen Page was quite sufficient. He had been working overtime and was treating himself to his first vacation in years - he was young - he was in love and he was very happy. Nor was there any question, either, that Helen Page was happy. Those who had known her since she was a child could not remember when she had not been happy, but these days she wore her joyousness with a difference. It was in her eyes, in her greetings to old friends: it showed itself hourly in courtesies and kindnesses. She was very kind to Latimer, too. She did not deceive him. She told him she liked better to be with him than with any one else, - it would have been difficult to deny to him what was apparent to an entire summer colony, - but she explained that that did not mean she would marry him. She announced this when the signs she knew made it seem necessary. She announced it in what was for her a roundabout way, by remarking suddenly that she did not intend to marry for several years.

This brought Latimer to his feet and called forth from him remarks so eloquent that Helen found it very difficult to keep her own. She as though she had been caught in an undertow and was being whirled out to sea. When, at last, she had regained her breath, only because Latimer had paused to catch his, she shook her head miserably.

" The trouble is, " she complained, "there are so many

think the same thing!"

"What do they think?" demanded Latimer.

"That they want to marry me."

Checked but not discouraged, Latimer attacked in force.

"I can quite believe that," he agreed, "but there's this important difference: no matter how much a man wants to marry you, he can't LOVE you as I do!"

"That's ANOTHER thing they think," sighed Helen.

"I'm sorry to be so unoriginal," snapped Latimer.

"PLEASE don't!" pleaded Helen. "I don't mean to be unfeeling. I'm not unfeeling. I'm only trying to be fair. If I don't seem to take it to heart, it's because I know it does no good. I can see how miserable a girl must be if she is loved by one man and can't make up her mind whether or not she wants to marry him. But when there's so many she just stops worrying; for she can't possibly marry them all."

"ALL!" exclaimed Latimer. "It is incredible that I have undervalued you, but may I ask how many there are?"

"I don't know," sighed Helen miserably. "There seems to be something about me that - "

"There is!" interrupted Latimer. "I've noticed it. You don't have to tell me about it. I know that the Helen Page habit is a damned difficult habit to break!"

It cannot be said that he made any violent effort to break it. At least, not one that was obvious to Fair Harbor or to Helen.

One of their favorite drives was through the pine woods to the point on which stood the lighthouse, and on one of these excursions they explored a forgotten wood road and came out upon a cliff. The cliff overlooked the sea, and below it was a jumble of rocks with which the waves played hide and seek. On many afternoons and mornings they returned to this place, and, while Latimer read to her, Helen would sit with her back to a tree and toss pine-cones into the water. Sometimes the poets whose works he read made love so charmingly that Latimer was most grateful to them for rendering such excellent first aid to the wounded, and into his voice he would throw all that feeling and music that from juries and mass meetings had dragged tears and cheers and votes.

But when his voice became so appealing that it no longer was possible for any woman to resist it, Helen would exclaim excitedly: "Please excuse me for interrupting, but there is a large spider - " and the spell was gone.

One day she exclaimed: "Oh!" and Latimer patiently lowered the "Oxford Book of Verse," and asked: "What is it, NOW?"

"I'm so sorry," Helen said, "but I can't help watching that Chapman boy; he's only got one reef in, and the next time he jibs he'll capsize, and he can't swim, and he'll drown. I told his mother only yesterday - "

"I haven't the least interest in the Chapman boy," said

Latimer, "or in what you told his mother, or whether he drowns or not! I'm a drowning man myself!"

Helen shook her head firmly and reprovingly. "Men get over THAT kind of drowning," she said.

"Not THIS kind of man doesn't!" said Latimer. "And don't tell me," he cried indignantly, "that that's ANOTHER thing they all say."

"If one could only be sure!" sighed Helen. "If one could only be sure that you - that the right man would keep on caring after you marry him the way he says he cares before you marry him. If you could know that, it would help you a lot in making up your mind."

"There is only one way to find that out," said Latimer; "that is to marry him. I mean, of course," he corrected hastily, "to marry me."

One day, when on their way to the cliff at the end of the wood road, the man who makes the Nantucket sailor and peddles him passed through the village; and Latimer bought the sailorman and carried him to their hiding-place. There he fastened him to the lowest limb of one of the ancient pine-trees that helped to screen their hiding-place from the world. The limb reached out free of the other branches, and the wind caught the sailorman fairly and spun him like a dancing dervish. Then it tired of him, and went off to try to drown the Chapman boy, leaving the sailorman motionless with his arms outstretched, balancing in each hand a tiny oar and smiling happily.

"He has a friendly smile," said Helen; "I think he likes us."

"He is on guard," Latimer explained. "I put him there to warn us if any one approaches, and when we are not here, he is to frighten away trespassers. Do you understand?" he demanded of the sailorman. "Your duty is to protect this beautiful lady. So long as I love her you must guard this place. It is a life sentence. You are always on watch. You never sleep. You are her slave. She says you have a friendly smile. She wrongs you. It is a beseeching, abject, worshipping smile. I am sure when I look at her mine is equally idiotic. In fact, we are in many ways alike. I also am her slave. I also am devoted only to her service. And I never sleep, at least not since I met her."

From her throne among the pine needles Helen looked up at the sailorman and frowned.

"It is not a happy simile," she objected. "For one thing, a sailorman has a sweetheart in every port."

"Wait and see," said Latimer.

"And," continued the girl with some asperity, "if there is anything on earth that changes its mind as often as a weather-vane, that is less CERTAIN, less CONSTANT - "

"Constant?" Latimer laughed at her in open scorn. "You come back here," he challenged, "months from now, years from now, when the winds have beaten him, and the sun blistered him, and the snow frozen him, and you will find him smiling at you just as he is now, just as confidently, proudly, joyously, devotedly. Because those who are your slaves, those who love YOU, cannot come to any harm; only if you disown them, only if you drive them away!

The sailorman, delighted at such beautiful language, threw himself about in a delirium of joy. His arms spun in their sockets like Indian clubs, his oars flashed in the sun, and his eyes and lips were fixed in one blissful, long-drawn-out, unalterable smile.

When the golden-rod turned gray, and the leaves red and yellow, and it was time for Latimer to return to his work in the West, he came to say good-by. But the best Helen could do to keep hope alive in him was to say that she was glad he cared. She added it was very helpful to think that a man such as he believed you were so fine a person, and during the coming winter she would try to be like the fine person he believed her to be, but which, she assured him, she was not.

Then he told her again she was the most wonderful being in the world, to which she said: "Oh, indeed no!" and then, as though he were giving her a cue, he said: "Good-by!" But she did not take up his cue, and they shook hands. He waited, hardly daring to breathe.

"Surely, now that the parting has come," he assured himself, "she will make some sign, she will give me a word, a look that will write 'total' under the hours we have spent together, that will help to carry me through the long winter."

But he held her hand so long and looked at her so hungrily that he really forced her to say: "Don't miss your train," which kind consideration for his comfort did not delight him as it should. Nor, indeed, later did she herself recall the remark with satisfaction.

With Latimer out of the way the other two hundred and forty-nine suitor attacked with renewed hope. Among other advantages they had over Latimer was that they were on the ground. They saw Helen daily, at dinners, dances, at the country clubs, in her own drawing-room. Like any sailor from the Charlestown Navy Yard and his sweetheart, they could walk beside her in the park and throw peanuts to the pigeons, and scratch dates and initials on the green benches; they could walk with her up one side of Commonwealth Avenue and down the south bank of the Charles, when the sun was gilding the dome of the State House, when the bridges were beginning to deck themselves with necklaces of lights. They had known her since they wore knickerbockers; and they shared many interests and friends in common; they talked the same language. Latimer could talk to her only in letters, for with her he shared no friends or interests, and he was forced to choose between telling her of his lawsuits and his efforts in politics or of his love. To write to her of his affairs seemed wasteful and impertinent, and of his love for her, after she had received what he told of it in silence, he was too proud to speak. So he wrote but seldom, and then only to say: "You know what I send you." Had he known it, his best letters were those he did not send. When in the morning mail Helen found his familiar handwriting, that seemed to stand out like the face of a friend in a crowd, she would pounce upon the letter, read it, and, assured of his love, would go on her way rejoicing. But when in the morning there was no letter, she wondered why, and all day she wondered why. And the next morning when again she was disappointed, her thoughts of Latimer and her doubts and speculations concerning him shut out every other interest. He became a perplexing, insistent problem. He was never out of her mind. And then he would spoil it all by writing her that he loved her and that of all the women in the world she was the only one. And, reassured upon that point, Helen happily and promptly would forget all about him.

But when she remembered him, although months had passed since she had seen him, she remembered him much more distinctly, much more gratefully, than that one of the two hundred and fifty with whom she had walked that same afternoon. Latimer could not know it, but of that anxious multitude he was first, and there was no second. At least Helen hoped, when she was ready to marry, she would love Latimer enough to want to marry him. But as yet she assured herself she did not want to marry any one. As she was, life was very satisfactory. Everybody loved her, everybody invited her to be of his party, or invited himself to join hers, and the object of each seemed to be to see that she enjoyed every hour of every day. Her nature was such that to make her happy was not difficult. Some of her devotees could do it by giving her a dance and letting her invite half of Boston, and her kid brother could do it by taking her to Cambridge to watch the team at practice.

She thought she was happy because she was free. As a matter of fact, she was happy because she loved some one and that particular some one loved her. Her being "free" was only her mistaken way of putting it. Had she thought she had lost Latimer and his love, she would have discovered that, so far from being free, she was bound hand and foot and heart and soul.

But she did not know that, and Latimer did not know that.

Meanwhile, from the branch of the tree in the sheltered, secret hiding-place that overlooked the ocean, the sailorman kept watch. The sun had blistered him, the storms had buffeted him, the snow had frozen upon his shoulders. But his loyalty never relaxed. He spun to the north, he spun to the south, and so rapidly did he scan the surrounding landscape that no one could hope to creep upon him unawares. Nor, indeed, did any one attempt to do so. Once a fox stole into the secret hiding-place, but the sailorman flapped his oars and frightened him away. He was always triumphant. To birds, to squirrels, to trespassing rabbits he was a thing of terror. Once, when the air was still, an impertinent crow perched on the very limb on which he stood, and with scornful, disapproving eyes surveyed his white trousers, his blue reefer, his red cheeks. But when the wind suddenly drove past them the sailorman sprang into action and the crow screamed in alarm and darted away. So, alone and with no one to come to his relief, the sailorman stood his watch. About him the branches bent with the snow, the icicles froze him into immobility, and in the tree-tops strange groanings filled him with alarms. But undaunted, month after month, alert and smiling, he waited the return of the beautiful lady and of the tall young man who had devoured her with such beseeching, unhappy eyes.

Latimer found that to love a woman like Helen Page as he loved her was the best thing that could come into his life. But to sit down and lament over the fact that she did not love him did not, to use his favorite expression, "tend toward efficiency." He removed from his sight the three pictures of her he had cut from illustrated papers, and ceased to write to her.

In his last letter he said: "I have told you how it is, and that is how it is always going to be. There never has been, there never can be any one but you. But my love is too precious, too sacred to be brought out every week in a letter and dangled before your eyes like an advertisement of a motor-car. It is too wonderful a thing to be cheapened, to be subjected to slights and silence. If ever you should want it, it is yours. It is here waiting. But you must tell me so. I have done everything a man can do to make you understand. But you do not want me or my love. And my love says to me: 'Don't send me there again to have the door shut in my face. Keep me with you to be your inspiration, to help you to live worthily.' And so it shall be."

When Helen read that letter she did not know what to do. She did not know how to answer it. Her first impression was that suddenly she had grown very old, and that some one had turned off the sun, and that in consequence the world had naturally grown cold and dark. She could not see why the two hundred and forty-nine expected her to keep on doing exactly the same things she had been doing with delight for six months, and indeed for the last six years. Why could they not see that no longer was there any pleasure in them? She would have written and told Latimer that she found she loved him very dearly if in her mind there had not arisen a fearful doubt. Suppose his letter was not quite honest? He said that he would always love her, but how could she now know that? Why might not this letter be only his way of withdrawing from a position which he wished to abandon, from which, perhaps, he was even glad to escape? Were this true, and she wrote and said all those things that were in her heart, that now she knew were true, might she not hold him to her against his will? The love that once he had for her might no longer exist, and if, in her turn, she told him she loved him and had always loved him, might he not in some mistaken spirit of chivalry feel it was his duty to pretend to care? Her cheeks burned at the thought. It was intolerable. She could not write that letter. And as day succeeded day, to do so became more difficult. And so she never wrote and was very unhappy. And Latimer was very unhappy. But he had his work, and Helen had none, and for her life became a game of putting little things together, like a picture puzzle, an hour here and an hour there, to make up each day. It was a dreary game.

From time to time she heard of him through the newspapers. For, in his own State, he was an "Insurgent" making a fight, the outcome of which was expected to show what might follow throughout the entire West. When he won his fight much more was written about him, and he became a national figure. In his own State the people hailed him as the next governor, promised him a seat in the Senate. To Helen this seemed to take him further out of her life. She wondered if now she held a place even in his thoughts.

At Fair Harbor the two hundred and forty-nine used to joke with her about her politician. Then they considered Latimer of importance only because Helen liked him. Now they discussed him impersonally and over her head, as though she were not present, as a power, an influence, as the leader and exponent of a new idea. They seemed to think she no longer could pretend to any peculiar claim upon him, that now he belonged to all of them.

Older men would say to her: "I hear you know Latimer? What sort of a man is he?"

Helen would not know what to tell them. She could not

say he was a man who sat with his back to a pine-tree, reading from a book of verse, or halting to devour her with humble, entreating eyes.

She went South for the winter, the doctors deciding she was run down and needed the change. And with an unhappy laugh at her own expense she agreed in their diagnosis. She was indifferent as to where they sent her, for she knew wherever she went she must still force herself to go on putting one hour on top of another, until she had built up the inexorable and necessary twenty-four.

When she returned winter was departing, but reluctantly, and returning unexpectedly to cover the world with snow, to eclipse the thin spring sunshine with cheerless clouds. Helen took herself seriously to task. She assured herself it was weak-minded to rebel. The summer was coming and Fair Harbor with all its old delights was before her. She compelled herself to take heart, to accept the fact that, after all, the world is a pretty good place, and that to think only of the past, to live only on memories and regrets, was not only cowardly and selfish, but, as Latimer had already decided, did not tend toward efficiency.

Among the other rules of conduct that she imposed upon herself was not to think of Latimer. At least, not during the waking hours. Should she, as it sometimes happened, dream of him - should she imagine they were again seated among the pines, riding across the downs, or racing at fifty miles an hour through country roads, with the stone fences flying past, with the wind and the sun in their eyes, and in their hearts happiness and content - that would not be breaking her rule. If she dreamed of him , she could not be held responsible. She could only be grateful.

And then, just as she had banished him entirely from her mind, he came East. Not as once he had planned to come, only to see her, but with a blare of trumpets, at the command of many citizens, as the guest of three cities. He was to speak at public meetings, to confer with party leaders, to carry the war into the enemy's country. He was due to speak in Boston at Faneuil Hall on the first of May, and that same night to leave for the West, and three days before his coming Helen fled from the city. He had spoken his message to Philadelphia, he had spoken to New York, and for a week the papers had spoken only of him. And for that week, from the sight of his printed name, from sketches of him exhorting cheering mobs, from snap-shots of him on rear platforms leaning forward to grasp eager hands, Helen had shut her eyes. And that during the time he was actually in Boston she might spare herself further and more direct attacks upon her feelings she escaped to Fair Harbor, there to remain until, on the first of May at midnight, he again would pass out of her life, maybe forever. No one saw in her going any significance. Spring had come, and in preparation for the summer season the house at Fair Harbor must be opened and set in order, and the presence there of some one of the Page family was easily explained.

She made the three hours' run to Fair Harbor in her car, driving it herself, and as the familiar landfalls fell into place, she doubted if it would not have been wiser had she stayed away. For she found that the memories of more than twenty summers at Fair Harbor had been wiped out by those of one summer, by those of one man. The natives greeted her joyously: the boatmen, the fishermen, her own grooms and gardeners, the village postmaster, the oldest inhabitant. They welcomed her as though they were her vassals and she their queen. But it was the one man she had exiled from Fair Harbor who at every turn wrung her heart and caused her throat to tighten. She passed the cottage where he had lodged, and hundreds of years seemed to have gone since she used to wait for him in the street, blowing noisily on her automobile horn, calling derisively to his open windows. Wherever she turned Fair Harbor spoke of him. The golf-links; the bathing beach; the ugly corner in the main street where he always reminded her that it was better to go slow for ten seconds than to remain a long time dead; the old house on the stone wharf where the schooners made fast, which he intended to borrow for his honeymoon; the wooden trough where they always drew rein to water the ponies; the pond into which he had waded to bring her lilies.

On the second day of her stay she found she was passing these places purposely, that to do so she was going out of her way. They no longer distressed her, but gave her a strange comfort. They were old friends, who had known her in the days when she was rich in happiness.

But the secret hiding-place - their very own hiding-place, the opening among the pines that overhung the jumble of rocks and the sea - she could not bring herself to visit. And then, on the afternoon of the third day when she was driving alone toward the lighthouse, her pony, of his own accord, from force of habit, turned smartly into the wood road. And again from force of habit, before he reached the spot that overlooked the sea, he came to a full stop. There was no need to make him fast. For hours, stretching over many summer days, he had stood under those same branches patiently waiting.

On foot, her heart beating tremulously, stepping reverently, as one enters the aisle of some dim cathedral, Helen advanced into the sacred circle. And then she stood quite still. What she had expected to find there she could not have told, but it was gone. The place was unknown to her. She saw an opening among gloomy pines, empty, silent, unreal. No haunted house, no barren moor, no neglected graveyard ever spoke more poignantly, more mournfully, with such utter hopelessness. There was no sign of his or of her former presence. Across the open space something had passed its hand, and it had changed. What had been a trysting-place, a bower, a nest, had become a tomb. A tomb, she felt, for something that once had been brave, fine, and beautiful, but which now was dead. She had but one desire, to escape from the place, to put it away from her forever, to remember it, not as she now found it, but as first she had remembered it, and as now she must always remember It. She turned softly on tiptoe as one who has intruded on a shrine.

But before she could escape there came from the sea a sudden gust of wind that caught her by the skirts and drew her back, that set the branches tossing and swept the dead leaves racing about her ankles. And at the same instant from just above her head there beat upon the air a violent, joyous tattoo - a sound that was neither of the sea nor of the woods, a creaking, swiftly repeated sound, like the flutter of caged wings.

Helen turned in alarm and raised her eyes - and beheld the sailorman.

Tossing his arms in a delirious welcome, waltzing in a frenzy of joy, calling her back to him with wild beckonings, she saw him smiling down at her with the same radiant, beseeching, worshipping smile. In Helen's ears Latimer's commands to the sailorman rang as clearly as though Latimer stood before her and had just spoken. Only now they were no longer a jest; they were a vow, a promise, an oath of allegiance that brought to her peace, and pride, and happiness.

"So long as I love this beautiful lady," had been his foolish words, "you will guard this place. It is a life sentence!"

With one hand Helen Page dragged down the branch on which the sailorman stood, with the other she snatched him from his post of duty. With a joyous laugh that was a sob, she clutched the sailorman in both her hands and kissed the beseeching, worshipping smile.

An hour later her car, on its way to Boston, passed through Fair Harbor at a rate of speed that caused her chauffeur to pray between his chattering teeth that the first policeman would save their lives by landing them in jail.

At the wheel, her shoulders thrown forward, her eyes searching the dark places beyond the reach of the leaping head-lights Helen Page raced against time, against the minions of the law, against sudden death, to beat the midnight train out of Boston, to assure the man she loved of the one thing that could make his life worth living.

And close against her heart, buttoned tight beneath her

great-coat, the sailorman smiled in the darkness, his long watch over, his soul at peace, his duty well performed.

Chapter 6.

THE MIND READER

When Philip Endicott was at Harvard, he wrote stories of undergraduate life suggested by things that had happened to himself and to men he knew. Under the title of "Tales of the Yard" they were collected in book form, and sold surprisingly well. After he was graduated and became a reporter on the New York Republic, he wrote more stories, in each of which a reporter was the hero, and in which his failure or success in gathering news supplied the plot. These appeared first in the magazines, and later in a book under the title of "Tales of the Streets." They also were well received.

Then came to him the literary editor of the Republic, and said: "There are two kinds of men who succeed in writing fiction - men of genius and reporters. A reporter can describe a thing he has seen in such a way that he can make the reader see it, too. A man of genius can describe something he has never seen, or any one else for that matter, in such a way that the reader will exclaim: 'I have never committed a murder; but if I had, that's just the way I'd feel about it.' For instance, Kipling tells us how a Greek pirate, chained to the oar of a trireme, suffers; how a mother rejoices when her baby crawls across her breast. Kipling has never been a mother or a pirate, but he convinces you he knows how each of them feels. He can do that because he is a genius; you cannot do it because you are not. At college you wrote only of what you saw at college; and now that you are in the newspaper business all your tales are only of newspaper work. You merely report what you see. So, if you are doomed to write only of what you see, then the best thing for you to do is to see as many things as possible. You must see all kinds of life. You must progress. You must leave New York, and you had better go to London."

"But on the Republic," Endicott pointed out, "I get a salary. And in London I should have to sweep a crossing."

"Then," said the literary editor, "you could write a story about a man who swept a crossing."

It was not alone the literary editor's words of wisdom that had driven Philip to London. Helen Carey was in London, visiting the daughter of the American Ambassador; and, though Philip had known her only one winter, he loved her dearly. The great trouble was that he had no money, and that she possessed so much of it that, unless he could show some unusual quality of mind or character, his asking her to marry him, from his own point of view at least, was quite impossible. Of course, he knew that no one could love her as he did, that no one so truly wished for her happiness, or would try so devotedly to make her happy. But to him it did not seem possible that a girl could be happy with a man who was not able to pay for her home, or her clothes, or her food, who would have to borrow her purse if he wanted a new pair of gloves or a hair-cut.

For Philip Endicott, while rich in birth and education and charm of manner, had no money at all. When, in May, he came from New York to lay siege to London and to the heart of Helen Carey he had with him, all told, fifteen hundred dollars. That was all he possessed in the world; and unless the magazines bought his stories there was no prospect of his getting any more.

Friends who knew London told him that, if you knew London well, it was easy to live comfortably there and to go about and even to entertain modestly on three sovereigns a day. So, at that rate, Philip calculated he could stay three months. But he found that to know London well enough to be able to live there on three sovereigns a day you had first to spend so many five-pound notes in getting acquainted with London that there were no sovereigns left. At the end of one month he had just enough money to buy him a second-class passage back to New York, and he was as far from Helen as ever.

Often he had read in stories and novels of men who were too poor to marry. And he had laughed at the idea. He had always said that when two people truly love each other it does not matter whether they have money or not. But when in London, with only a five-pound note, and face to face with the actual proposition of asking Helen Carey not only to marry him but to support him, he felt that money counted for more than he had supposed. He found money was many different things - it was self-respect, and proper pride, and private honors and independence. And, lacking these things, he felt he could ask no girl to marry him, certainly not one for whom he cared as he cared for Helen Carey. Besides, while he knew how he loved her, he had no knowledge whatsoever that she loved him. She always seemed extremely glad to see him; but that might be explained in different ways. It might be that what was in her heart for him was really a sort of "old home week" feeling; that to her it was a relief to see any one who spoke her own language, who did not need to have it explained when she was jesting, and who did not think when she was speaking in perfectly satisfactory phrases that she must be talking slang.

The Ambassador and his wife had been very kind to Endicott, and, as a friend of Helen's, had asked him often to dinner and had sent him cards for dances at which Helen was to be one of the belles and beauties. And Helen herself had been most kind, and had taken early morning walks with him in Hyde Park and through the National Galleries; and they had fed buns to the bears in the Zoo, and in doing so had laughed heartily. They thought it was because the bears were so ridiculous that they laughed. Later they appreciated that the reason they were happy was because they were together. Had the bear pit been empty, they still would have laughed.

On the evening of the thirty-first of May, Endicott had gone to bed with his ticket purchased for America and his last five-pound note to last him until the boat sailed. He was a miserable young man. He knew now that he loved Helen Carey in such a way that to put the ocean between them was liable to unseat his courage and his self-control. In London he could, each night, walk through Carlton House Terrace and, leaning against the iron rails of the Carlton Club, gaze up at her window. But, once on the other side of the ocean, that tender exercise must be abandoned. He must even consider her pursued by most attractive guardsmen, diplomats, and belted earls. He knew they could not love her as he did; he knew they could not love her for the reasons he loved her, because the fine and beautiful things in her that he saw and worshipped they did not seek, and so did not find. And yet, for lack of a few thousand dollars, he must remain silent, must put from him the best that ever came into his life, must waste the wonderful devotion he longed to give, must starve the love that he could never summon for any other woman.

On the thirty-first of May he went to sleep utterly and completely miserable. On the first of June he woke hopeless and unrefreshed.

And then the miracle came.

Prichard, the ex-butler who valeted all the young gentlemen in the house where Philip had taken chambers, brought him his breakfast. As he placed the eggs and muffins on the tables to Philip it seemed as though Prichard had said: "I am sorry he is leaving us. The next gentleman who takes these rooms may not be so open-handed. He never locked up his cigars or his whiskey. I wish he'd give me his old dress-coat. It fits me, except across the shoulders."

Philip stared hard at Prichard; but the lips of the valet had not moved. In surprise and bewilderment, Philip demanded:

"How do you know it fits? Have you tried it on?"

"I wouldn't take such a liberty," protested Prichard. "Not with any of our gentlemen's clothes."

"How did you know I was talking about clothes," demanded Philip. "You didn't say anything about clothes, did you?"

"No, sir, I did not; but you asked me, sir, and I - "

"Were you thinking of clothes?"

"Well, sir, you might say, in a way, that I was, answered the valet. "Seeing as you're leaving, sir, and they're not over-new, I thought "

"It's mental telepathy," said Philip.

"I beg your pardon," exclaimed Prichard.

"You needn't wait," said Philip.

The coincidence puzzled him; but by the time he had read the morning papers he had forgotten about it, and it was not until he had emerged into the street that it was forcibly recalled. The street was crowded with people; and as Philip stepped in among them, It was as though every one at whom he looked began to talk aloud. Their lips did not move, nor did any sound issue from between them; but, without ceasing, broken phrases of thoughts came to him as clearly as when, in passing in a crowd, snatches of talk are carried to the ears. One man thought of his debts; another of the weather, and of what disaster it might bring to his silk hat; another planned his luncheon; another was rejoicing over a telegram he had but that moment received. To himself he kept repeating the words of the telegram - "No need to come, out of danger." To Philip the message came as clearly as though he were reading it from the folded slip of paper that the stranger clutched in his hand.

Confused and somewhat frightened, and in order that undisturbed he might consider what had befallen him, Philip sought refuge from the crowded street in the hallway of a building. His first thought was that for some unaccountable cause his brain for the moment was playing tricks with him, and he was inventing the phrases he seemed to hear, that he was attributing thoughts to others of which they were entirely innocent. But, whatever it was that had befallen him, he knew it was imperative that he should at once get at the meaning of it.

The hallway in which he stood opened from Bond Street up a flight of stairs to the studio of a fashionable photographer, and directly in front of the hallway a young woman of charming appearance had halted. Her glance was troubled, her manner ill at ease. To herself she kept repeating: "Did I tell Hudson to be here at a quarter to eleven, or a quarter past? Will she get the telephone message to bring the ruff? Without the ruff it would be absurd to be photographed. Without her ruff Mary Queen of Scots would look ridiculous!"

Although the young woman had spoken not a single word, although indeed she was biting impatiently at her lower lip, Philip had distinguished the words clearly. Or, if he had not distinguished them, he surely was going mad. It was a matter to be at once determined, and the young woman should determine it. He advanced boldly to her, and raised his hat.

"Pardon me," he said, "but I believe you are waiting for your maid Hudson?"

As though fearing an impertinence, the girl regarded him in silence.

"I only wish to make sure," continued Philip, "that you are she for whom I have a message. You have an appointment, I believe, to be photographed in fancy dress as Mary Queen of Scots?"

"Well?" assented the girl.

"And you telephoned Hudson," he continued, "to bring you your muff."

The girl exclaimed with vexation.

"Oh!" she protested; "I knew they'd get it wrong! Not muff, ruff! I want my ruff."

Philip felt a cold shiver creep down his spine.

"For the love of Heaven!" he exclaimed in horror; "it's true!"

"What's true?" demanded the young woman in some alarm.

"That I'm a mind reader," declared Philip. "I've read your mind! I can read everybody's mind. I know just what you're thinking now. You're thinking I'm mad!"

The actions of the young lady showed that again he was correct. With a gasp of terror she fled past him and raced up the stairs to the studio. Philip made no effort to follow and to explain. What was there to explain? How could he explain that which, to himself, was unbelievable? Besides, the girl had served her purpose.

If he could read the mind of one, he could read the minds of all. By some unexplainable miracle, to his ordinary equipment of senses a sixth had been added. As easily as, before that morning, he could look into the face of a fellow-mortal, he now could look into the workings of that fellow-mortal's mind. The thought was appalling. It was like living with one's ear to a key-hole. In his dismay his first idea was to seek medical advice - the best in London. He turned instantly in the direction of Harley Street. There, he determined, to the most skilled alienist in town he would explain his strange plight. For only as a misfortune did the miracle appear to him. But as he made his way through the streets his pace slackened.

Was he wise, he asked himself, in allowing others to know he possessed this strange power? Would they not at once treat him as a madman? Might they not place him under observation, or even deprive him of his liberty? At the thought he came to an abrupt halt His own definition of the miracle as a "power" had opened a new line of speculation. If this strange gift (already he was beginning to consider it more leniently) were concealed from others, could he not honorably put it to some useful purpose? For, among the blind, the man with one eye is a god. Was not he - among all other men the only one able to read the minds of all other men - a god? Turning into Bruton Street, he paced its quiet length considering the possibilities that lay within him.

It was apparent that the gift would lead to countless embarrassments. If it were once known that he possessed it, would not even his friends avoid him? For how could any one, knowing his most secret thought was at the mercy of another, be happy in that other's presence? His power would lead to his social ostracism. Indeed, he could see that his gift might easily become a curse. He decided not to act hastily, that for the present he had best give no hint to others of his unique power.

As the idea of possessing this power became more familiar, he regarded it with less aversion. He began to consider to what advantage he could place it. He could see that, given the right time and the right man, he might learn secrets leading to far-reaching results. To a statesman, to a financier, such a gift as he possessed would make him a ruler of men. Philip had no desire to be a ruler of men; but he asked himself how could he bend this gift to serve his own? What he most wished was to marry Helen Carey; and, to that end, to possess money. So he must meet men who possessed money, who were making money. He would put questions to them. And with words they would give evasive answers; but their minds would tell him the truth.

The ethics of this procedure greatly disturbed him. Certainly it was no better than reading other people's letters. But, he argued, the dishonor in knowledge so obtained would lie only in the use he made of it. If he used it without harm to him from whom it was obtained and with benefit to others, was he not justified in trading on his superior equipment? He decided that each case must be considered separately in accordance with the principle involved. But, principle or no principle, he was determined to become rich. Did not the end justify the means? Certainly an all-wise Providence had not brought Helen Carey into his life only to take her away from him. It could not be so cruel. But, in selecting them for one another, the all-wise Providence had overlooked the fact that she was rich and he was poor. For that oversight Providence apparently was now endeavoring to make amends. In what certainly was a fantastic and roundabout manner Providence had tardily equipped him with a gift that could lead to great wealth. And who was he to fly in the face of Providence? He decided to set about building up a fortune, and building it in a hurry.

From Bruton Street he had emerged upon Berkeley Square; and, as Lady Woodcote had invited him to meet Helen at luncheon at the Ritz, he turned in that direction. He was too early for luncheon; but in the corridor of the Ritz he knew he would find persons of position and fortune, and in reading their minds he might pass the time before luncheon with entertainment, possibly with profit. For, while pacing Bruton Street trying to discover the principles of conduct that threatened to hamper his new power, he had found that in actual operation it was quite simple. He learned that his mind, in relation to other minds, was like the receiver of a wireless station with an unlimited field. For, while the wireless could receive messages only from those instruments with which it was attuned, his mind was in key with all other minds. To read the thoughts of another, he had only to concentrate his own upon that person; and to shut off the thoughts of that person, he had only to turn his own thoughts elsewhere. But also he discovered that over the thoughts of those outside the range of his physical sight he had no control. When he asked of what Helen Carey was at that moment thinking, there was no result. But when he asked, "Of what is that policeman on the corner thinking?" he was surprised to find that that officer of the law was formulating regulations to abolish the hobble skirt as an impediment to traffic.

As Philip turned into Berkeley Square, the accents of a mind in great distress smote upon his new and sixth sense. And, in the person of a young gentleman leaning against the park railing, he discovered the source from which the mental sufferings emanated. The young man was a pink-cheeked, yellow-haired youth of extremely boyish appearance, and dressed as if for the race-track. But at the moment his pink and babyish face wore an expression of complete misery. With tear-filled eyes he was gazing at a house of yellow stucco on the opposite side of the street. And his thoughts were these: "She is the best that ever lived, and I am the most ungrateful of fools. How happy were we in the house of yellow stucco! Only now, when she has closed its doors to me, do I know how happy! If she would give me another chance, never again would I distress or deceive her."

So far had the young man progressed in his thoughts when an automobile of surprising smartness swept around the corner and drew up in front of the house of yellow stucco, and from it descended a charming young person. She was of the Dresden-shepherdess type, with large blue eyes of haunting beauty and innocence.

"My wife!" exclaimed the blond youth at the railings. And instantly he dodged behind a horse that, while still attached to a four-wheeler, was contentedly eating from a nose-bag.

With a key the Dresden shepherdess opened the door to the yellow house and disappeared.

The calling of the reporter trains him in audacity, and to act quickly. He shares the troubles of so many people that to the troubles of other people he becomes callous, and often will rush in where friends of the family fear to tread. Although Philip was not now acting as a reporter, he acted quickly. Hardly had the door closed upon the young lady than he had mounted the steps and rung the visitor's bell. As he did so, he could not resist casting a triumphant glance in the direction of the outlawed husband. And, in turn, what the outcast husband, peering from across the back of the cab horse, thought of Philip, of his clothes, of his general appearance, and of the manner in which he would delight to alter all of them, was quickly communicated to the American. They were thoughts of a nature so violent and uncomplimentary that Philip hastily cut off all connection.

As Philip did not know the name of the Dresden-china doll, it was fortunate that on opening the door, the butler promptly announced:

"Her ladyship is not receiving."

"Her ladyship will, I think, receive me," said Philip pleasantly, "when you tell her I come as the special ambassador of his lordship."

From a tiny reception-room on the right of the entrance-hall there issued a feminine exclamation of surprise, not unmixed with joy; and in the hall the noble lady instantly appeared.

When she saw herself confronted by a stranger, she halted in embarrassment. But as, even while she halted, her only thought had been, "Oh! if he will only ask me to forgive him!" Philip felt no embarrassment whatsoever. Outside, concealed behind a cab horse, was the erring but bitterly repentant husband; inside, her tenderest thoughts racing tumultuously toward him, was an unhappy child-wife begging to be begged to pardon.

For a New York reporter, and a Harvard graduate of charm and good manners, it was too easy.

"I do not know you," said her ladyship. But even as she spoke she motioned to the butler to go away. "You must be one of his new friends." Her tone was one of envy.

"Indeed, I am his newest friend," Philip assured her; "but I can safely say no one knows his thoughts as well as I. And they are all of you!"

The china shepherdess blushed with happiness, but instantly she shook her head.

"They tell me I must not believe him," she announced. "They tell me - "

"Never mind what they tell you," commanded Philip. "Listen to ME. He loves you. Better than ever before, he loves you. All he asks is the chance to tell you so. You cannot help but believe him. Who can look at you, and not believe that he loves you! Let me," he begged, "bring him to you." He started from her when, remembering the somewhat violent thoughts of the youthful husband, he added hastily: "Or perhaps it would be better if you called him yourself."

"Called him!" exclaimed the lady. "He is in Paris-at the races - with her!"

" If they tell you that sort of thing," protested Philip

indignantly, "you must listen to me. He is not in Paris. He is not with her. There never was a her!"

He drew aside the lace curtains and pointed. "He is there - behind that ancient cab horse, praying that you will let him tell you that not only did he never do it; but, what is much more important, he will never do it again."

The lady herself now timidly drew the curtains apart, and then more boldly showed herself upon the iron balcony. Leaning over the scarlet geraniums, she beckoned with both hands. The result was instantaneous. Philip bolted for the front door, leaving it open; and, as he darted down the steps, the youthful husband, in strides resembling those of an ostrich, shot past him. Philip did not cease running until he was well out of Berkeley Square. Then, not ill-pleased with the adventure, he turned and smiled back at the house of yellow stucco.

"Bless you, my children," he murmured; "bless you!"

He continued to the Ritz; and, on crossing Piccadilly to the quieter entrance to the hotel in Arlington Street, found gathered around it a considerable crowd drawn up on either side of a red carpet that stretched down the steps of the hotel to a court carriage. A red carpet in June, when all is dry under foot and the sun is shining gently, can mean only royalty; and in the rear of the men in the street Philip halted. He remembered that for a few days the young King of Asturia and the Queen Mother were at the Ritz incognito; and, as he never had seen the young man who so recently and so tragically had been exiled from his own kingdom, Philip raised himself on tiptoe and stared expectantly.

As easily as he could read their faces could he read the thoughts of those about him. They were thoughts of friendly curiosity, of pity for the exiles; on the part of the policemen who had hastened from a cross street, of pride at their temporary responsibility; on the part of the coachman of the court carriage, of speculation as to the possible amount of his Majesty's tip. The thoughts were as harmless and protecting as the warm sunshine.

And then, suddenly and harshly, like the stroke of a fire bell at midnight, the harmonious chorus of gentle, hospitable thoughts was shattered by one that was discordant, evil, menacing. It was the thought of a man with a brain diseased; and its purpose was murder.

"When they appear at the doorway," spoke the brain of the maniac, "I shall lift the bomb from my pocket. I shall raise it above my head. I shall crash it against the stone steps. It will hurl them and all of these people into eternity and me with them. But I shall LIVE - a martyr to the Cause. And the Cause will flourish!"

Through the unsuspecting crowd, like a football player diving for a tackle, Philip hurled himself upon a little dark man standing close to the open door of the court carriage. From the rear Philip seized him around the waist and locked his arms behind him, elbow to elbow. Philip's face, appearing over the man's shoulder, stared straight into that of the policeman.

"He has a bomb in his right-hand pocket!" yelled Philip. "I can hold him while you take it! But, for Heaven's sake, don't drop it!" Philip turned upon the crowd. "Run! all of you!" he shouted. "Run like the devil!"

At that instant the boy King and his Queen Mother, herself still young and beautiful, and cloaked with a dignity and sorrow that her robes of mourning could not intensify, appeared in the doorway.

"Go back, sir!" warned Philip. "He means to kill you!"

At the words and at sight of the struggling men, the great lady swayed helplessly, her eyes filled with terror. Her son sprang protectingly in front of her. But the danger was past. A second policeman was now holding the maniac by the wrists, forcing his arms above his head; Philip's arms, like a lariat, were wound around his chest; and from his pocket the first policeman gingerly drew forth a round, black object of the size of a glass fire-grenade. He held it high in the air, and waved his free hand warningly. But the warning was unobserved. There was no one remaining to observe it. Leaving the would-be assassin struggling and biting in the grasp of the stalwart policeman, and the other policeman unhappily holding the bomb at arm's length, Philip sought to escape into the Ritz. But the young King broke through the circle of attendants and stopped him.

"I must thank you," said the boy eagerly; "and I wish you to tell me how you came to suspect the man's purpose."

Unable to speak the truth, Philip, the would-be writer of fiction, began to improvise fluently.

"To learn their purpose, sir," he said, "is my business. I am of the International Police, and in the secret service of your Majesty."

"Then I must know your name," said the King, and added with a dignity that was most becoming, "You will find we are not ungrateful."

Philip smiled mysteriously and shook his head.

"I said in your secret service," he repeated. "Did even your Majesty know me, my usefulness would be at an end." He pointed toward the two policemen. "If you desire to be just, as well as gracious, those are the men to reward."

He slipped past the King and through the crowd of hotel officials into the hall and on into the corridor.

The arrest had taken place so quietly and so quickly that through the heavy glass doors no sound had penetrated, and of the fact that they had been so close to a possible tragedy those in the corridor were still ignorant. The members of the Hungarian orchestra were arranging their music; a waiter was serving two men of middle age with sherry; and two distinguished-looking elderly gentlemen seated together on a sofa were talking in leisurely whispers.

One of the two middle-aged men was well known to Philip, who as a reporter had often, in New York, endeavored to interview him on matters concerning the steel trust. His name was Faust. He was a Pennsylvania Dutchman from Pittsburgh, and at one time had been a foreman of the night shift in the same mills he now controlled. But with a roar and a spectacular flash, not unlike one of his own blast furnaces, he had soared to fame and fortune. He recognized Philip as one of the bright young men of the Republic; but in his own opinion he was far too self-important to betray that fact.

Philip sank into an imitation Louis Quatorze chair beside a fountain in imitation of one in the apartment of the Pompadour, and ordered what he knew would be an execrable imitation of an American cocktail. While waiting for the cocktail and Lady Woodcote's luncheon party, Philip, from where he sat, could not help but overhear the conversation of Faust and of the man with him. The latter was a German with Hebraic features and a pointed beard. In loud tones he was congratulating the American many-time millionaire on having that morning come into possession of a rare and valuable masterpiece, a hitherto unknown and but recently discovered portrait of Philip IV by Velasquez.

Philip sighed enviously.

"Fancy," he thought, "owning a Velasquez! Fancy having it all to yourself! It must be fun to be rich. It certainly is hell to be poor!"

The German, who was evidently a picture-dealer, was exclaiming in tones of rapture, and nodding his head with an air of awe and solemnity.

"I am telling you the truth, Mr. Faust," he said. "In no gallery in Europe, no, not even in the Prado, is there such another Velasquez. This is what you are doing, Mr. Faust, you are robbing Spain. You are robbing her of something worth more to her than Cuba. And I tell you, so soon as it is known that this Velasquez is going to your home in Pittsburgh, every Spaniard will hate you and every art-collector will hate you, too. For it is the most wonderful art treasure in Europe. And what a bargain, Mr. Faust! What a bargain!"

To make sure that the reporter was within hearing, Mr. Faust glanced in the direction of Philip and, seeing that he had heard, frowned importantly. That the reporter might hear still more, he also raised his voice.

"Nothing can be called a bargain, Baron," he said, "that costs three hundred thousand dollars!"

Again he could not resist glancing toward Philip, and so eagerly that Philip deemed it would be only polite to look interested. So he obligingly assumed a startled look, with which he endeavored to mingle simulations of surprise, awe, and envy.

The next instant an expression of real surprise overspread his features.

Mr. Faust continued. "If you will come upstairs," he said to the picture-dealer, "I will give you your check; and then I should like to drive to your apartments and take a farewell look at the picture."

"I am sorry," the Baron said, "but I have had it moved to my art gallery to be packed."

"Then let's go to the gallery," urged the patron of art. "We've just time before lunch." He rose to his feet, and on the instant the soul of the picture-dealer was filled with alarm.

In actual words he said: "The picture is already boxed and in its lead coffin. No doubt by now it is on its way to Liverpool. I am sorry." But his thoughts, as Philip easily read them, were: "Fancy my letting this vulgar fool into the Tate Street workshop! Even HE would know that old masters are not found in a half-finished state on Chelsea-made frames and canvases. Fancy my letting him see those two half-completed Van Dycks, the new Hals, the half-dozen Corots. He would even see his own copy of Velasquez next to the one exactly like it - the one MacMillan finished yesterday and that I am sending to Oporto, where next year, in a convent, we shall 'discover' it."

Philip's surprise gave way to intense amusement. In his delight at the situation upon which he had stumbled, he laughed aloud. The two men, who had risen, surprised at the spectacle of a young man laughing at nothing, turned and stared. Philip also rose.

"Pardon me," he said to Faust, "but you spoke so loud I couldn't help overhearing. I think we've met before, when I was a reporter on the Republic."

The Pittsburgh millionaire made a pretense, of annoyance.

"Really!" he protested irritably, "you reporters butt in everywhere. No public man is safe. Is there no place we can go where you fellows won't annoy us?"

"You can go to the devil for all I care," said Philip, "or even to Pittsburgh!"

He saw the waiter bearing down upon him with the imitation cocktail, and moved to meet it. The millionaire, fearing the reporter would escape him, hastily changed his tone. He spoke with effective resignation.

"However, since you've learned so much," he said, "I'll tell you the whole of it. I don't want the fact garbled, for it is of international importance. Do you know what a Velasquez is?"

"Do you?" asked Philip.

The millionaire smiled tolerantly.

"I think I do," he said. "And to prove it, I shall tell you something that will be news to you. I have just bought a Velasquez that I am going to place in my art museum. It is worth three hundred thousand dollars."

Philip accepted the cocktail the waiter presented. It was quite as bad as he had expected.

"Now, I shall tell you something," he said, "that will be news to you. You are not buying a Velasquez. It is no more a Velasquez than this hair oil is a real cocktail. It is a bad copy, worth a few dollars."

"How dare you!" shouted Faust. "Are you mad?"

The face of the German turned crimson with rage.

"Who is this insolent one?" he sputtered.

"I will make you a sporting proposition," said Philip. "You can take it, or leave it. You two will get into a taxi. You will drive to this man's studio in Tate Street. You will find your Velasquez is there and not on its way to Liverpool. And you will find one exactly like it, and a dozen other 'old masters' half-finished. I'll bet you a hundred pounds I'm right! And I'll bet this man a hundred pounds that he DOESN'T DARE TAKE YOU TO HIS STUDIO!"

"Indeed, I will not," roared the German. "It would be to insult myself."

"It would be an easy way to earn a hundred pounds, too," said Philip.

"How dare you insult the Baron?" demanded Faust. "What makes you think - "

"I don't think, I know!" said Philip. "For the price of a taxi-cab fare to Tate Street, you win a hundred pounds."

"We will all three go at once," cried the German. "My car is outside. Wait here. I will have it brought to the door?"

Faust protested indignantly.

"Do not disturb yourself, Baron," he said; "just because a fresh reporter - "

But already the German had reached the hall. Nor did he stop there. They saw him, without his hat, rush into Piccadilly, spring into a taxi, and shout excitedly to the driver. The next moment he had disappeared.

"That's the last you'll see of him," said Philip.

"His actions are certainly peculiar," gasped the millionaire. "He did not wait for us. He didn't even wait for his hat! I think, after all, I had better go to Tate Street."

"Do so," said Philip, "and save yourself three hundred thousand dollars, and from the laughter of two continents. You'll find me here at lunch. If I'm wrong, I'll pay you a hundred pounds."

"You should come with me," said Faust. "It is only fair to yourself."

"I'll take your word for what you find in the studio," said Philip. "I cannot go. This is my busy day."

Without further words, the millionaire collected his hat and stick, and, in his turn, entered a taxi-cab and disappeared.

Philip returned to the Louis Quatorze chair and lit a cigarette. Save for the two elderly gentlemen on the sofa, the lounge was still empty, and his reflections were undisturbed. He shook his head sadly.

"Surely," Philip thought, "the French chap was right who said words were given us to conceal our thoughts. What a strange world it would be if every one possessed my power. Deception would be quite futile and lying would become a lost art. I wonder," he mused cynically, "is any one quite honest? Does any one speak as he thinks and think as he speaks?"

At once came a direct answer to his question. The two elderly gentlemen had risen and, before separating, had halted a few feet from him.

"I sincerely hope, Sir John," said one of the two, "that you have no regrets. I hope you believe that I have advised you in the best interests of all?"

"I do, indeed," the other replied heartily "We shall be thought entirely selfish; but you know and I know that what we have done is for the benefit of the shareholders."

Philip was pleased to find that the thoughts of each of the old gentlemen ran hand in hand with his spoken words. "Here, at least," he said to himself, "are two honest men."

As though loath to part, the two gentlemen still lingered.

"And I hope," continued the one addressed as Sir John, "that you approve of my holding back the public announcement of the combine until the afternoon. It will give the shareholders a better chance. Had we given out the news in this morning's papers the stockbrokers would have - "

"It was most wise," interrupted the other. "Most just."

The one called Sir John bowed himself away, leaving the other still standing at the steps of the lounge. With his hands behind his back, his chin sunk on his chest, he remained, gazing at nothing, his thoughts far away.

Philip found them thoughts of curious interest. They were concerned with three flags. Now, the gentleman considered them separately; and Philip saw the emblems painted clearly in colors, fluttering and flattened by the breeze. Again, the gentleman considered them in various combinations; but always, in whatever order his mind arranged them, of the three his heart spoke always to the same flag, as the heart of a mother reaches toward her firstborn.

Then the thoughts were diverted; and in his mind's eye

the old gentleman was watching the launching of a little schooner from a shipyard on the Clyde. At her main flew one of the three flags - a flag with a red cross on a white ground. With thoughts tender and grateful, he followed her to strange, hot ports, through hurricanes and tidal waves; he saw her return again and again to the London docks, laden with odorous coffee, mahogany, red rubber, and raw bullion. He saw sister ships follow in her wake to every port in the South Sea; saw steam packets take the place of the ships with sails; saw the steam packets give way to great ocean liners, each a floating village, each equipped, as no village is equipped, with a giant power house, thousands of electric lamps, suite after suite of silk-lined boudoirs, with the floating harps that vibrate to a love message three hundred miles away, to the fierce call for help from a sinking ship. But at the main of each great vessel there still flew the same house-flag - the red cross on the field of white - only now in the arms of the cross there nestled proudly a royal crown.

Philip cast a scared glance at the old gentleman, and raced down the corridor to the telephone.

Of all the young Englishmen he knew, Maddox was his best friend and a stock-broker. In that latter capacity Philip had never before addressed him. Now he demanded his instant presence at the telephone.

Maddox greeted him genially, but Philip cut him short.

"I want you to act for me," he whispered, "and act quick! I want you to buy for me one thousand shares of the Royal Mail Line, of the Elder-Dempster, and of the Union Castle."

He heard Maddox laugh indulgently.

"There's nothing in that yarn of a combine," he called. "It has fallen through. Besides, shares are at fifteen pounds."

Philip, having in his possession a second-class ticket and a five-pound note, was indifferent to that, and said so.

"I don't care what they are," he shouted. "The combine is already signed and sealed, and no one knows it but myself. In an hour everybody will know it!"

"What makes you think you know it?" demanded the broker.

"I've seen the house-flags!" cried Philip. "I have - do as I tell you," he commanded.

There was a distracting delay.

"No matter who's back of you," objected Maddox, "it's a big order on a gamble."

"It's not a gamble," cried Philip. "It's an accomplished fact. I'm at the Ritz. Call me up there. Start buying now, and, when you've got a thousand of each, stop!"

Philip was much too agitated to go far from the telephone booth; so for half an hour he sat in the reading-room, forcing himself to read the illustrated papers. When he found he had read the same advertisement five times, he returned to the telephone. The telephone boy met him half-way with a message.

"Have secured for you a thousand shares of each," he read, "at fifteen. Maddox."

Like a man awakening from a nightmare, Philip tried to separate the horror of the situation from the cold fact. The cold fact was sufficiently horrible. It was that, without a penny to pay for them, he had bought shares in three steamship lines, which shares, added together, were worth two hundred and twenty five thousand dollars. He returned down the corridor toward the lounge. Trembling at his own audacity, he was in a state of almost complete panic, when that happened which made his outrageous speculation of little consequence. It was drawing near to half-past one; and, in the persons of several smart men and beautiful ladies, the component parts of different luncheon parties were beginning to assemble.

Of the luncheon to which Lady Woodcote had invited him, only one guest had arrived; but, so far as Philip was concerned, that one was sufficient. It was Helen herself, seated alone, with her eyes fixed on the doors opening from Piccadilly. Philip, his heart singing with appeals, blessings, and adoration, ran toward her. Her profile was toward him, and she could not see him; but he could see her. And he noted that, as though seeking some one, her eyes were turned searchingly upon each young man as he entered and moved from one to another of those already in the lounge. Her expression was eager and anxious.

"If only," Philip exclaimed, "she were looking for me! She certainly is looking for some man. I wonder who it can be?"

As suddenly as if he had slapped his face into a wall,

he halted in his steps. Why should he wonder? Why did he not read her mind? Why did he not KNOW? A waiter was hastening toward him. Philip fixed his mind upon the waiter, and his eyes as well. Mentally Philip demanded of him: "Of what are you thinking?"

There was no response. And then, seeing an unlit cigarette hanging from Philip's lips, the waiter hastily struck a match and proffered it. Obviously, his mind had worked, first, in observing the half-burned cigarette; next, in furnishing the necessary match. And of no step in that mental process had Philip been conscious! The conclusion was only too apparent. His power was gone. No longer was he a mind reader!

Hastily Philip reviewed the adventures of the morning. As he considered them, the moral was obvious. The moment he had used his power to his own advantage, he had lost it. So long as he had exerted it for the happiness of the two lovers, to save the life of the King, to thwart the dishonesty of a swindler, he had been all-powerful; but when he endeavored to bend it to his own uses, it had fled from him. As he stood abashed and repentant, Helen turned her eyes toward him; and, at the sight of him, there leaped to them happiness and welcome and complete content. It was "the look that never was on land or sea," and it was not necessary to be a mind reader to understand it. Philip sprang toward her as quickly as a man dodges a taxi-cab.

"I came early," said Helen, "because I wanted to talk to you before the others arrived." She seemed to be repeating words already rehearsed, to be following a course of conduct already predetermined. "I want to tell you," she said, "that I am sorry you are going away. I want to tell you that I shall miss you very much." She paused and drew a long breath. And she looked at Philip as if she was begging him to make it easier for her to go on.

Philip proceeded to make it easier.

"Will you miss me," he asked, "in the Row, where I used to wait among the trees to see you ride past? Will you miss me at dances, where I used to hide behind the dowagers to watch you waltzing by? Will you miss me at night, when you come home by sunrise, and I am not hiding against the railings of the Carlton Club, just to see you run across the pavement from your carriage, just to see the light on your window blind, just to see the light go out, and to know that you are sleeping?"

Helen's eyes were smiling happily. She looked away from him.

"Did you use to do that?" she asked.

"Every night I do that," said Philip. "Ask the policemen! They arrested me three times."

"Why?" said Helen gently.

But Philip was not yet free to speak, so he said:

"They thought I was a burglar."

Helen frowned. He was making it very hard for her.

"You know what I mean," she said. "Why did you keep guard outside my window?"

"It was the policeman kept guard," said Philip. "I was there only as a burglar. I came to rob. But I was a coward, or else I had a conscience, or else I knew my own unworthiness." There was a long pause. As both of them, whenever they heard the tune afterward, always remembered, the Hungarian band, with rare inconsequence, was playing the "Grizzly Bear," and people were trying to speak to Helen. By her they were received with a look of so complete a lack of recognition, and by Philip with a glare of such savage hate, that they retreated in dismay. The pause seemed to last for many years.

At last Helen said: "Do you know the story of the two roses? They grew in a garden under a lady's window. They both loved her. One looked up at her from the ground and sighed for her; but the other climbed to the lady's window, and she lifted him in and kissed him - because he had dared to climb."

Philip took out his watch and looked at it. But Helen did not mind his doing that, because she saw that his eyes were filled with tears. She was delighted to find that she was making it very hard for him, too.

"At any moment," Philip said, "I may know whether I owe two hundred and twenty-five thousand dollars which I can never pay, or whether I am worth about that sum. I should like to continue this conversation at the exact place where you last spoke - AFTER I know whether I am going to jail, or whether I am worth a quarter of a million dollars."

Helen laughed aloud with happiness.

" I knew that was it!" she cried. "You don't like my

money. I was afraid you did not like ME. If you dislike my money, I will give it away, or I will give it to you to keep for me. The money does not matter, so long as you don't dislike me."

What Philip would have said to that, Helen could not know, for a page in many buttons rushed at him with a message from the telephone, and with a hand that trembled Philip snatched it. It read: "Combine is announced, shares have gone to thirty-one, shall I hold or sell?"

That at such a crisis he should permit of any interruption hurt Helen deeply. She regarded him with unhappy eyes. Philip read the message three times. At last, and not without uneasy doubts as to his own sanity, he grasped the preposterous truth. He was worth almost a quarter of a million dollars! At the page he shoved his last and only five-pound note. He pushed the boy from him.

"Run!" he commanded. "Get out of here, Tell him he is to SELL!"

He turned to Helen with a look in his eyes that could not be questioned or denied. He seemed incapable of speech, and, to break the silence, Helen said: "Is it good news?"

"That depends entirely upon you," replied Philip soberly. "Indeed, all my future life depends upon what you are going to say next."

Helen breathed deeply and happily.

"And - what am I going to say?"

"How can I know that?" demanded Philip. "Am I a mind reader?"

But what she said may be safely guessed from the fact that they both chucked Lady Woodcotes luncheon, and ate one of penny buns, which they shared with the bears in Regents Park.

Philip was just able to pay for the penny buns. Helen paid for the taxi-cab.

Chapter 7.

THE NAKED MAN

In their home town of Keepsburg, the Keeps were the reigning dynasty, socially and in every way. Old man Keep was president of the trolley line, the telephone company, and the Keep National Bank. But Fred, his son, and the heir apparent, did not inherit the business ability of his father; or, if he did, he took pains to conceal that fact. Fred had gone through Harvard, but as to that also, unless he told people, they would not have known it. Ten minutes after Fred met a man he generally told him.

When Fred arranged an alliance with Winnie Platt, who also was of the innermost inner set of Keepsburg, everybody said Keepsburg would soon lose them. And everybody was right. When single, each had sighed for other social worlds to conquer, and when they combined their fortunes and ambitions they found Keepsburg impossible, and they left it to lay siege to New York. They were too crafty to at once attack New York itself. A widow lady they met while on their honeymoon at Palm Beach had told them not to attempt that. And she was the Palm Beach correspondent of a society paper they naturally accepted her advice. She warned them that in New York the waiting-list is already interminable, and that, if you hoped to break into New York society, the clever thing to do was to lay siege to it by way of the suburbs and the country clubs. If you went direct to New York knowing no one, you would at once expose that fact, and the result would be disastrous.

She told them of a couple like themselves, young and rich and from the West, who, at the first dance to which they were invited, asked, "Who is the old lady in the wig?" and that question argued them so unknown that it set them back two years. It was a terrible story, and it filled the Keeps with misgivings. They agreed with the lady correspondent that it was far better to advance leisurely; first firmly to intrench themselves in the suburbs, and then to enter New York, not as the Keeps from Keepsburg, which meant nothing, but as the Fred Keeps of Long Island, or Westchester, or Bordentown.

"In all of those places," explained the widow lady, "our smartest people have country homes, and at the country club you may get to know them. Then, when winter comes, you follow them on to the city."

The point from which the Keeps elected to launch their attack was Scarboro-on-the-Hudson. They selected Scarboro because both of them could play golf, and they planned that their first skirmish should be fought and won upon the golf-links of the Sleepy Hollow Country Club. But the attack did not succeed. Something went wrong. They began to fear that the lady correspondent had given them the wrong dope. For, although three months had passed, and they had played golf together until they were as loath to clasp a golf club as a red-hot poker, they knew no one, and no one knew them. That is, they did not know the Van

Wardens; and if you lived at Scarboro and were not recognized by the Van Wardens, you were not to be found on any map.

Since the days of Hendrik Hudson the country-seat of the Van Wardens had looked down upon the river that bears his name, and ever since those days the Van Wardens had looked down upon everybody else. They were so proud that at all their gates they had placed signs reading, "No horses allowed. Take the other road." The other road was an earth road used by tradespeople from Ossining; the road reserved for the Van Wardens, and automobiles, was of bluestone. It helped greatly to give the Van Warden estate the appearance of a well kept cemetery. And those Van Wardens who occupied the country-place were as cold and unsociable as the sort of people who occupy cemeteries - except "Harry" Van Warden, and she lived in New York at the Turf Club.

Harry, according to all local tradition - for he frequently motored out to Warden Koopf, the Van Warden country-seat - and, according to the newspapers, was a devil of a fellow and in no sense cold or unsociable. So far as the Keeps read of him, he was always being arrested for overspeeding, or breaking his collar-bone out hunting, or losing his front teeth at polo. This greatly annoyed the proud sisters at Warden Koopf; not because Harry was arrested or had broken his collar-bone, but because it dragged the family name into the newspapers.

"If you would only play polo or ride to hounds instead of playing golf," sighed Winnie Keep to her husband, "you would meet Harry Van Warden, and he'd introduce you to his sisters, and then we could break in anywhere."

"If I was to ride to hounds," returned her husband, "the only thing I'd break would be my neck."

The country-place of the Keeps was completely satisfactory, and for the purposes of their social comedy the stage-setting was perfect. The house was one they had rented from a man of charming taste and inflated fortune; and with it they had taken over his well-disciplined butler, his pictures, furniture, family silver, and linen. It stood upon an eminence, was heavily wooded, and surrounded by many gardens; but its chief attraction was an artificial lake well stocked with trout that lay directly below the terrace of the house and also in full view from the road to Albany.

This latter fact caused Winnie Keep much concern. In the neighborhood were many Italian laborers, and on several nights the fish had tempted these born poachers to trespass; and more than once, on hot summer evenings, small boys from Tarrytown and Ossining had broken through the hedge, and used the lake as a swimming-pool.

"It makes me nervous," complained Winnie. "I don't like the idea of people prowling around so near the house. And think of those twelve hundred convicts, not one mile away, in Sing Sing. Most of them are burglars, and if they ever get out, our house is the very first one they'll break into."

"I haven't caught anybody in this neighborhood breaking into our house yet," said Fred, "and I'd be glad to see even a burglar!"

They were seated on the brick terrace that overlooked the lake. It was just before the dinner hour, and the dusk of a wonderful October night had fallen on the hedges, the clumps of evergreens, the rows of close-clipped box. A full moon was just showing itself above the tree-tops, turning the lake into moving silver. Fred rose from his wicker chair and, crossing to his young bride, touched her hair fearfully with the tips of his fingers.

"What if we don't know anybody, Win," he said, "and nobody knows us? It's been a perfectly good honey-moon, hasn't it? If you just look at it that way, it works out all right. We came here really for our honeymoon, to be together, to be alone - "

Winnie laughed shortly. "They certainly have left us alone!" she sighed.

"But where else could we have been any happier?" demanded the young husband loyally. "Where will you find any prettier place than this, just as it is at this minute, so still and sweet and silent? There's nothing the matter with that moon, is there? Nothing the matter with the lake? Where's there a better place for a honeymoon? It's a bower - a bower of peace, solitude a - bower of - "

As though mocking his words, there burst upon the sleeping countryside the shriek of a giant siren. It was raucous, virulent, insulting. It came as sharply as a scream of terror, it continued in a bellow of rage. Then, as suddenly as it had cried aloud, it sank to silence; only after a pause of an instant, as though giving a signal, to shriek again in two sharp blasts. And then again it broke into the hideous long drawn scream of rage, insistent, breathless, commanding; filling the soul of him who heard it, even of the innocent, with alarm.

"In the name of Heaven!" gasped Keep, "what's that?"

Down the terrace the butler was hastening toward them. When he stopped, he spoke as though he were announcing dinner. "A convict, sir," he said, "has escaped from Sing Sing. I thought you might not understand the whistle. I thought perhaps you would wish Mrs. Keep to come in-doors."

"Why?" asked Winnie Keep.

"The house is near the road, madam," said the butler. "And there are so many trees and bushes. Last summer two of them hid here, and the keepers - there was a fight." The man glanced at Keep. Fred touched his wife on the arm.

"It's time to dress for dinner, Win," he said.

"And what are you going to do?" demanded Winnie.

I'm going to finish this cigar first. It doesn't take me long to change." He turned to the butler. "And I'll have a cocktail, too I'll have it out here."

The servant left them, but in the French window that opened from the terrace to the library Mrs. Keep lingered irresolutely. "Fred," she begged, "you - you're not going to poke around in the bushes, are you? - just because you think I'm frightened?"

Her husband laughed at her. "I certainly am NOT!" he said. "And you're not frightened, either. Go in. I'll be with you in a minute."

But the girl hesitated. Still shattering the silence of the night the siren shrieked relentlessly; it seemed to be at their very door, to beat and buffet the window-panes. The bride shivered and held her fingers to her ears.

"Why don't they stop it!" she whispered. "Why don't they give him a chance!"

When she had gone, Fred pulled one of the wicker chairs to the edge of the terrace, and, leaning forward with his chin in his hands, sat staring down at the lake. The moon had cleared the tops of the trees, had blotted the lawns with black, rigid squares, had disguised the hedges with wavering shadows. Somewhere near at hand a criminal - a murderer, burglar, thug - was at large, and the voice of the prison he had tricked still bellowed in rage, in amazement, still clamored not only for his person but perhaps for his life. The whole countryside heard it: the farmers bedding down their cattle for the night; the guests of the Briar Cliff Inn, dining under red candle shades; the joy riders from the city, racing their cars along the Albany road. It woke the echoes of Sleepy Hollow. It crossed the Hudson. The granite walls of the Palisades flung it back against the granite walls of the prison. Whichever way the convict turned, it hunted him, reaching for him, pointing him out - stirring in the heart of each who heard it the lust of the hunter, which never is so cruel as when the hunted thing is a man.

"Find him!" shrieked the siren. "Find him! He's there, behind your hedge! He's kneeling by the stone wall. THAT'S he running in the moonlight. THAT'S he crawling through the dead leaves! Stop him! Drag him down! He's mine! Mine!"

But from within the prison, from within the gray walls that made the home of the siren, each of twelve hundred men cursed it with his soul. Each, clinging to the bars of his cell, each, trembling with a fearful joy, each, his thumbs up, urging on with all the strength of his will the hunted, rat-like figure that stumbled panting through the crisp October night, bewildered by strange lights, beset by shadows, staggering and falling, running like a mad dog in circles, knowing that wherever his feet led him the siren still held him by the heels.

As a rule, when Winnie Keep was dressing for dinner, Fred, in the room adjoining, could hear her unconsciously and light-heartedly singing to herself. It was a habit of hers that he loved. But on this night, although her room was directly above where he sat upon the terrace, he heard no singing. He had been on the terrace for a quarter of an hour. Gridley, the aged butler who was rented with the house, and who for twenty years had been an inmate of it, had brought the cocktail and taken away the empty glass. And Keep had been alone with his thoughts. They were entirely of the convict. If the man suddenly confronted him and begged his aid, what would he do? He knew quite well what he would do. He considered even the means by which he would assist the fugitive to a successful get-away.

The ethics of the question did not concern Fred. He did not weigh his duty to the State of New York, or to society. One day, when he had visited "the institution," as a somewhat sensitive neighborhood prefers to speak of it, he was told that the chance of a prisoner's escaping from Sing Sing and not being at once retaken was one out of six thousand. So with Fred it was largely a sporting proposition. Any man who could beat a six-thousand-to-one shot commanded his admiration.

And, having settled his own course of action, he tried to imagine himself in the place of the man who at that very moment was endeavoring to escape. Were he that man, he would first, he decided, rid himself of his tell-tale clothing. But that would leave him naked, and in Westchester County a naked man would be quite as conspicuous as one in the purple-gray cloth of the prison. How could he obtain clothes? He might hold up a passer-by, and, if the passer-by did not flee from him or punch him into insensibility, he might effect an exchange of garments; he might by threats obtain them from some farmer; he might despoil a scarecrow.

But with none of these plans was Fred entirely satisfied. The question deeply perplexed him. How best could a naked man clothe himself? And as he sat pondering that point, from the bushes a naked man emerged. He was not entirely undraped. For around his nakedness he had drawn a canvas awning. Fred recognized it as having been torn from one of the row-boats in the lake. But, except for that, the man was naked to his heels. He was a young man of Fred's own age. His hair was cut close, his face smooth-shaven, and above his eye was a half-healed bruise. He had the sharp, clever, rat-like face of one who lived by evil knowledge. Water dripped from him, and either for that reason or from fright the young man trembled, and, like one who had been running, breathed in short, hard gasps.

Fred was surprised to find that he was not in the least surprised. It was as though he had been waiting for the man, as though it had been an appointment.

Two thoughts alone concerned him: that before he could rid himself of his visitor his wife might return and take alarm, and that the man, not knowing his friendly intentions, and in a state to commit murder, might rush him. But the stranger made no hostile move, and for a moment in the moonlight the two young men eyed each other warily.

Then, taking breath and with a violent effort to stop the chattering of his teeth, the stranger launched into his story.

"I took a bath in your pond," he blurted forth, "and - and they stole my clothes! That's why I'm like this!"

Fred was consumed with envy. In comparison with this ingenious narrative how prosaic and commonplace became his own plans to rid himself of accusing garments and explain his nakedness. He regarded the stranger with admiration. But even though he applauded the other's invention, he could not let him suppose that he was deceived by it.

"Isn't it rather a cold night to take a bath?" he said.

As though in hearty agreement, the naked man burst into a violent fit of shivering.

"It wasn't a bath," he gasped. "It was a bet!"

"A what!" exclaimed Fred. His admiration was increasing. "A bet? Then you are not alone?"

"I am NOW - damn them!" exclaimed the naked one. He began again reluctantly. "We saw you from the road, you and a woman, sitting here in the light from that room. They bet me I didn't dare strip and swim across your pond with you sitting so near. I can see now it was framed up on me from the start. For when I was swimming back I saw them run to where I'd left my clothes, and then I heard them crank up, and when I got to the hedge the car was gone!"

Keep smiled encouragingly. "The car!" he assented. "So you've been riding around in the moonlight?"

The other nodded, and was about to speak when there burst in upon them the roaring scream of the siren. The note now was of deeper rage, and came in greater volume. Between his clinched teeth the naked one cursed fiercely, and then, as though to avoid further questions, burst into a fit of coughing. Trembling and shaking, he drew the canvas cloak closer to him. But at no time did his anxious, prying eyes leave the eyes of Keep.

"You - you couldn't lend me a suit of clothes could you?" he stuttered. "Just for to-night? I'll send them back. It's all right," he added; reassuringly. "I live near here."

With a start Keep raised his eyes, and distressed by his look, the young man continued less confidently.

"I don't blame you if you don't believe it," he stammered, "seeing me like this; but I DO live right near here. Everybody around here knows me, and I guess you've read about me in the papers, too. I'm - that is, my name - " like one about to take a plunge he drew a short breath, and the rat-like eyes regarded Keep watchfully - "my name is Van Warden. I'm the one you read about - Harry - I'm Harry Van Warden!"

After a pause, slowly and reprovingly Fred shook his head; but his smile was kindly even regretful, as though he were sorry he could not longer enjoy the stranger's confidences.

"My boy!" he exclaimed, "you're MORE than Van Warden! You're a genius!" He rose and made a peremptory gesture. "Sorry," he said, "but this isn't safe for either of us. Follow me, and I'll dress you up and send you where you want to go." He turned and whispered over his shoulder: "Some day let me hear from you. A man with your nerve - "

In alarm the naked one with a gesture commanded silence.

The library led to the front hall. In this was the coat-room. First making sure the library and hall were free of servants, Fred tiptoed to the coat-room and, opening the door, switched: on the electric light. The naked man, leaving in his wake a trail of damp footprints, followed at his heels.

Fred pointed at golf-capes, sweaters, greatcoats hanging from hooks, and on the floor at boots and overshoes.

"Put on that motor-coat and the galoshes," he commanded. "They'll cover you in case you have to run for it. I'm going to leave you here while I get you some clothes. If any of the servants butt in, don't lose your head. Just say you're waiting to see me - Mr.

Keep. I won't be long. Wait."

"Wait!" snorted the stranger. "You BET I'll wait!'

As Fred closed the door upon him, the naked one was rubbing himself violently with Mrs. Keep's yellow golf-jacket.

In his own room Fred collected a suit of blue serge, a tennis shirt, boots, even a tie. Underclothes he found ready laid out for him, and he snatched them from the bed. From a roll of money in his bureau drawer he counted out a hundred dollars. Tactfully he slipped the money in the trousers pocket of the serge suit and with the bundle of clothes in his arms raced downstairs and shoved them into the coat-room.

"Don't come out until I knock," he commanded. "And," he added in a vehement whisper, "don't come out at all unless you have clothes on!"

The stranger grunted.

Fred rang for Gridley and told him to have his car brought around to the door. He wanted it to start at once within two minutes. When the butler had departed, Fred, by an inch, again opened the coat-room door. The stranger had draped himself in the under-clothes and the shirt, and at the moment was carefully arranging the tie.

"Hurry!" commanded Keep. "The car'll be here in a minute. Where shall I tell him to take you?"

The stranger chuckled excitedly; his confidence seemed to be returning. "New York," he whispered, "fast as he can get there! Look here," he added doubtfully, "there's a roll of bills in these clothes."

"They're yours," said Fred.

The stranger exclaimed vigorously. "You're all right!" he whispered. "I won't forget this, or you either. I'll send the money back same time I send the clothes."

"Exactly!" said Fred.

The wheels of the touring-car crunched on the gravel drive, and Fred slammed to the door, and like a sentry on guard paced before it. After a period which seemed to stretch over many minutes there came from the inside a cautious knocking. With equal caution Fred opened the door of the width of a finger, and put his ear to the crack.

"You couldn't find me a button-hook, could you?" whispered the stranger.

Indignantly Fred shut the door and, walking to the veranda, hailed the chauffeur. James, the chauffeur, was a Keepsburg boy, and when Keep had gone to Cambridge James had accompanied him. Keep knew the boy could be trusted.

"You're to take a man to New York," he said, "or wherever he wants to go. Don't talk to him. Don't ask any questions. So, if YOU'RE questioned, you can say you know nothing. That's for your own good!"

The chauffeur mechanically touched his cap and started down the steps. As he did so, the prison whistle, still unsatisfied, still demanding its prey, shattered the silence. As though it had hit him a physical blow, the youth jumped. He turned and lifted startled, inquiring eyes to where Keep stood above him.

"I told you," said Keep, "to ask no questions.

As Fred re-entered the hall, Winnie Keep was coming down the stairs toward him. She had changed to one of the prettiest evening gowns of her trousseau, and so outrageously lovely was the combination of herself and the gown that her husband's excitement and anxiety fell from him, and he was lost in admiration. But he was not for long lost. To his horror; the door of the coat-closet opened toward his wife and out of the closet the stranger emerged. Winnie, not accustomed to seeing young men suddenly appear from among the dust-coats, uttered a sharp shriek.

With what he considered great presence of mind, Fred swung upon the visitor

"Did you fix it?" he demanded.

The visitor did not heed him. In amazement in abject admiration, his eyes were fastened upon the beautiful and radiant vision presented by Winnie Keep. But he also still preserved sufficient presence of mind to nod his head dully.

"Come," commanded Fred. "The car is waiting."

Still the stranger did not move. As though he had never before seen a woman, as though her dazzling loveliness held him in a trance, he stood still, gazing, gaping, devouring Winnie with his eyes. In her turn, Winnie beheld a strange youth who looked like a groom out of livery, so overcome by her mere presence as to be struck motionless and inarticulate. For protection she moved in some alarm toward her husband.

The stranger gave a sudden jerk of his body that might have been intended for a bow. Before Keep could interrupt him, like a parrot reciting its lesson, he exclaimed explosively:

"My name's Van Warden. I'm Harry Van Warden."

He seemed as little convinced of the truth of his statement as though he had announced that he was the Czar of Russia. It was as though a stage-manager had drilled him in the lines.

But upon Winnie, as her husband saw to his dismay, the words produced an instant and appalling effect. She fairly radiated excitement and delight. How her husband had succeeded in capturing the social prize of Scarboro she could not imagine, but, for doing so, she flashed toward him a glance of deep and grateful devotion.

Then she beamed upon the stranger. "Won't Mr. Van Warden stay to dinner?" she asked.

Her husband emitted a howl. "He will NOT!" he cried. "He's not that kind of a Van Warden. He's a plumber. He's the man that fixes the telephone!"

He seized the visitor by the sleeve of the long motor-coat and dragged him down the steps. Reluctantly, almost resistingly, the visitor stumbled after him, casting backward amazed glances at the beautiful lady.

Fred thrust him into the seat beside the chauffeur. Pointing at the golf-cap and automobile goggles which the stranger was stupidly twisting in his hands, Fred whispered fiercely:

"Put those on! Cover your face! Don't speak! The man knows what to do."

With eager eyes and parted lips James the chauffeur was waiting for the signal. Fred nodded sharply, and the chauffeur stooped to throw in the clutch. But the car did not start. From the hedge beside the driveway, directly in front of the wheels, something on all fours threw itself upon the gravel; something in a suit of purple-gray; something torn and bleeding, smeared with sweat and dirt; something that cringed and crawled, that tried to rise and sank back upon its knees, lifting to the glare of the head-lights the white face and white hair of a very old, old man. The kneeling figure sobbed; the sobs rising from far down in the pit of the stomach, wrenching the body like waves of nausea. The man stretched his arms toward them. From long disuse his voice cracked and broke.

"I'm done!" he sobbed. "I can't go no farther! I give myself up!"

Above the awful silence that held the four young people, the prison siren shrieked in one long, mocking howl of triumph.

It was the stranger who was the first to act. Pushing past Fred, and slipping from his own shoulders the long motor-coat, he flung it over the suit of purple-gray. The goggles he clapped upon the old man's frightened eyes, the golf-cap he pulled down over the white hair. With one arm he lifted the convict, and with the other dragged and pushed him into the seat beside the chauffeur. Into the hands of the chauffeur he thrust the roll of bills.

"Get him away!" he ordered. "It's only twelve miles to the Connecticut line. As soon as you're across, buy him clothes and a ticket to Boston. Go through White Plains to Greenwich - and then you're safe!"

As though suddenly remembering the presence of the owner of the car, he swung upon Fred. "Am I right?" he demanded.

"Of course!" roared Fred. He flung his arm at the chauffeur as though throwing him into space.

"Get-to-hell-out-of-here!" he shouted.

The chauffeur, by profession a criminal, but by birth a human being, chuckled savagely and this time threw in the clutch. With a grinding of gravel the racing-car leaped into the night, its ruby rear lamp winking in farewell, its tiny siren answering the great siren of the prison in jeering notes of joy and victory.

Fred had supposed that at the last moment the younger convict proposed to leap to the running-board, but instead the stranger remained motionless.

Fred shouted impotently after the flying car. In dismay he seized the stranger by the arm.

"But you?" he demanded. "How are you going to get away?"

The stranger turned appealingly to where upon the upper step stood Winnie Keep.

"I don't want to get away," he said. "I was hoping, maybe, you'd let me stay to dinner."

A terrible and icy chill crept down the spine of Fred Keep. He moved so that the light from the hall fell full upon the face of the stranger.

"Will you kindly tell me," Fred demanded, "who the devil you are?"

The stranger exclaimed peevishly. "I've BEEN telling you all evening," he protested. "I'm Harry Van Warden!"

Gridley, the ancient butler, appeared in the open door.

"Dinner is served, madam," he said.

The stranger gave an exclamation of pleasure. "Hello, Gridley!" he cried. "Will you please tell Mr. Keep who I am? Tell him, if he'll ask me to dinner, I won't steal the spoons."

Upon the face of Gridley appeared a smile it never had been the privilege of Fred Keep to behold. The butler beamed upon the stranger fondly, proudly, by the right of long acquaintanceship, with the affection of an old friend. Still beaming, he bowed to Keep.

"If Mr. Harry - Mr. Van Warden," he said, "is to stay to dinner, might I suggest, sir, he is very partial to the Paul Vibert, '84."

Fred Keep gazed stupidly from his butler to the stranger and then at his wife. She was again radiantly beautiful and smilingly happy.

Gridley coughed tentatively. "Shall I open a bottle, sir?" he asked.

Hopelessly Fred tossed his arms heavenward.

"Open a case!" he roared.

At ten o'clock, when they were still at table and reaching a state of such mutual appreciation that soon they would be calling each other by their first names, Gridley brought in a written message he had taken from the telephone. It was a long-distance call from Yonkers, sent by James, the faithful chauffeur.

Fred read it aloud.

"I got that party the articles he needed," it read, "and saw him safe on a train to Boston. On the way back I got arrested for speeding the car on the way down. Please send money. I am in a cell in Yonkers."

Chapter 8.

THE BOY WHO CRIED WOLF

Before he finally arrested him, "Jimmie" Sniffen had seen the man with the golf-cap, and the blue eyes that laughed at you, three times. Twice, unexpectedly, he had come upon him in a wood road and once on Round Hill where the stranger was pretending to watch the sunset. Jimmie knew people do not climb hills merely to look at sunsets, so he was not deceived. He guessed the man was a German spy seeking gun sites, and secretly vowed to "stalk" him. From that moment, had the stranger known it, he was as good as dead. For a boy scout with badges on his sleeve for "stalking" and "path-finding," not to boast of others for "gardening" and "cooking," can outwit any spy. Even had, General Baden-Powell remained in Mafeking and not invented the boy scout, Jimmie Sniffen would have been one. Because, by birth he was a boy, and by inheritance, a scout. In Westchester County the Sniffens are one of the county families. If it isn't a Sarles, it's a Sniffen; and with Brundages, Platts, and Jays, the Sniffens date back to when the acres of the first Charles Ferris ran from the Boston post road to the coach road to Albany, and when the first Gouverneur Morris stood on one of his hills and saw the Indian canoes in the Hudson and in the Sound and rejoiced that all the land between belonged to him.

If you do not believe in heredity, the fact that Jimmie's great-great-grandfather was a scout for General Washington and hunted deer, and even bear, over exactly the same hills where Jimmie hunted weasles will count for nothing. It will not explain why to Jimmie, from Tarrytown to Port Chester, the hills, the roads, the woods, and the cow-paths, caves, streams, and springs hidden in the woods were as familiar as his own kitchen garden,

Nor explain why, when you could not see a Pease and Elliman "For Sale" sign nailed to a tree, Jimmie could see in the highest branches a last year's bird's nest.

Or why, when he was out alone playing Indians and had sunk his scout's axe into a fallen log and then scalped the log, he felt that once before in those same woods he had trailed that same Indian, and with his own tomahawk split open his skull. Sometimes when he knelt to drink at a secret spring in the forest, the autumn leaves would crackle and he would raise his eyes fearing to see a panther facing him.

But there ain't no panthers in Westchester," Jimmie would reassure himself. And in the distance the roar of an automobile climbing a hill with the muffler open would seem to suggest he was right. But still Jimmie remembered once before he had knelt at that same spring, and that when he raised his eyes he had faced a crouching panther. "Mebbe dad told me it happened to grandpop," Jimmie would explain, "or I dreamed it, or, mebbe, I read it in a story book."

The "German spy" mania attacked Round Hill after the visit to the boy scouts of Clavering Gould, the war correspondent. He was spending the week end with

"Squire" Harry Van Vorst, and as young Van Vorst, besides being a justice of the peace and a Master of Beagles and President of the Country Club, was also a local "councilman" for the Round Hill Scouts, he brought his guest to a camp-fire meeting to talk to them. In deference to his audience, Gould told them of the boy scouts he had seen in Belgium and of the part they were playing in the great war. It was his peroration that made trouble.

"And any day," he assured his audience, "this country may be at war with Germany; and every one of you boys will be expected to do his bit. You can begin now. When the Germans land it will be near New Haven, or New Bedford. They will first capture the munition works at Springfield, Hartford, and Watervliet so as to make sure of their ammunition, and then they will start for New York City. They will follow the New Haven and New York Central railroads, and march straight through this village. I haven't the least doubt," exclaimed the enthusiastic war prophet, "that at this moment German spies are as thick in Westchester as blackberries. They are here to select camp sites and gun positions, to find out which of these hills enfilade the others and to learn to what extent their armies can live on the country. They are counting the cows, the horses, the barns where fodder is stored; and they are marking down on their maps the wells and streams."

As though at that moment a German spy might be crouching behind the door, Mr. Gould spoke in a whisper. "Keep your eyes open!" he commanded. "Watch every stranger. If he acts suspiciously, get word quick to your sheriff, or to Judge Van Vorst here. Remember the scouts' motto, 'Be prepared!'"

That night as the scouts walked home, behind each wall and hayrick they saw spiked helmets.

Young Van Vorst was extremely annoyed.

"Next time you talk to my scouts," he declared, you'll talk on 'Votes for Women.' After what you said to-night every real estate agent who dares open a map will be arrested. We're not trying to drive people away from Westchester, we're trying to sell them building sites."

"YOU are not!" retorted his friend, "you own half the county now, and you're trying to buy the other half."

"I'm a justice of the peace," explained Van Vorst. "I don't know WHY I am, except that they wished it on me. All I get out of it is trouble. The Italians make charges against my best friends for overspeeding and I have to fine them, and my best friends bring charges against the Italians for poaching, and when I fine the Italians, they send me Black Hand letters. And now every day I'll be asked to issue a warrant for a German spy who is selecting gun sites. And he will turn out to be a millionaire who is tired of living at the Ritz-Carlton and wants to 'own his own home' and his own golf-links. And he'll be so hot at being arrested that he'll take his millions to Long Island and try to break into the Piping Rock Club. And, it will be your fault!"

The young justice of the peace was right. At least so far as Jimmie Sniffen was concerned, the words of the war prophet had filled one mind with unrest. In the past Jimmie's idea of a holiday had been to spend it scouting in the woods. In this pleasure he was selfish. He did not want companions who talked, and trampled upon the dead leaves so that they frightened the wild animals and gave the Indians warning. Jimmie liked to pretend. He liked to fill the woods with wary and hostile adversaries. It was a game of his own inventing. If he crept to the top of a hill and on peering over it, surprised a fat woodchuck, he pretended the woodchuck was a bear, weighing two hundred pounds; if, himself unobserved, he could lie and watch, off its guard, a rabbit, squirrel, or, most difficult of all, a crow, it became a deer and that night at supper Jimmie made believe he was eating venison. Sometimes he was a scout of the Continental Army and carried despatches to General Washington. The rules of that game were that if any man ploughing in the fields, or cutting trees in the woods, or even approaching along the same road, saw Jimmie before Jimmie saw him, Jimmie was taken prisoner, and before sunrise was shot as a spy. He was seldom shot. Or else why on his sleeve was the badge for "stalking." But always to have to make believe became monotonous. Even "dry shopping" along the Rue de la Paix when you pretend you can have anything you see in any window, leaves one just as rich, but unsatisfied. So the advice of the war correspondent to seek out German spies came to Jimmie like a day at the circus, like a week at the Danbury Fair. It not only was a call to arms, to protect his flag and home, but a chance to play in earnest the game in which he most delighted. No longer need he pretend. No longer need he waste his energies in watching, unobserved, a greedy rabbit rob a carrot field. The game now was his fellow-man and his enemy; not only his enemy, but the enemy of his country.

In his first effort Jimmie was not entirely successful. The man looked the part perfectly; he wore an auburn beard, disguising spectacles, and he carried a suspicious knapsack. But he turned out to be a professor from the Museum of Natural History, who wanted to dig for Indian arrow-heads. And when Jimmie threatened to arrest him, the indignant gentleman arrested Jimmie. Jimmie escaped only by leading the professor to a secret cave of his own, though on some one else's property, where one not only could dig for arrow-heads, but find them. The professor was delighted, but for Jimmie it was a great disappointment. The week following Jimmie was again disappointed.

On the bank of the Kensico Reservoir, he came upon a man who was acting in a mysterious and suspicious manner. He was making notes in a book, and his runabout which he had concealed in a wood road was stuffed with blue-prints. It did not take Jimmie long to guess his purpose. He was planning to blow up the Kensico dam, and cut off the water supply of New York City. Seven millions of people without water! With out firing a shot, New York must surrender! At the thought Jimmie shuddered, and at the risk of his life by clinging to the tail of a motor truck, he followed the runabout into White Plains. But there it developed the mysterious stranger, so far from wishing to destroy the Kensico dam, was the State Engineer who had built it, and, also, a large part of the Panama Canal. Nor in his third effort was Jimmie more successful. From the heights of Pound Ridge he discovered on a hilltop below him a man working alone upon a basin of concrete. The man was a German-American, and already on Jimmie's list of "suspects." That for the use of the German artillery he was preparing a concrete bed for a siege gun was only too evident. But closer investigation proved that the concrete was only two inches thick. And the hyphenated one explained that the basin was built over a spring, in the waters of which he planned to erect a fountain and raise gold fish. It was a bitter blow. Jimmie became discouraged. Meeting Judge Van Vorst one day in the road he told him his troubles. The young judge proved unsympathetic. "My advice to you, Jimmie," he said, "is to go slow. Accusing everybody of espionage is a very serious matter. If you call a man a spy, it's sometimes hard for him to disprove it; and the name sticks. So, go slow - very slow. Before you arrest any more people, come to me first for a warrant."

So, the next time Jimmie proceeded with caution.

Besides being a farmer in a small way, Jimmie's father was a handy man with tools. He had no union card, but, in laying shingles along a blue chalk line, few were as expert. It was August, there was no school, and Jimmie was carrying a dinner-pail to where his father was at work on a new barn. He made a cross-cut through the woods, and came upon the young man in the golf-cap. The stranger nodded, and his eyes, which seemed to be always laughing, smiled pleasantly. But he was deeply tanned, and, from the waist up, held himself like a soldier, so, at once, Jimmie mistrusted him. Early the next morning Jimmie met him again. It had not been raining, but the clothes of the young man were damp. Jimmie guessed that while the dew was still on the leaves the young man had been forcing his way through underbrush. The stranger must have remembered Jimmie, for he laughed and exclaimed:

"Ah, my friend with the dinner-pail! It's luck you haven't got it now, or I'd hold you up. I'm starving!"

Jimmie smiled in sympathy. "It's early to be hungry," said Jimmie; "when did you have your breakfast?"

"I didn't," laughed the young man. "I went out to walk up an appetite, and I lost myself. But, I haven't lost my appetite. Which is the shortest way back to Bedford?"

"The first road to your right," said Jimmie.

"Is it far?" asked the stranger anxiously. That he was very hungry was evident.

"It's a half-hour's walk," said Jimmie

"If I live that long," corrected the young man; and stepped out briskly.

Jimmie knew that within a hundred yards a turn in the road would shut him from sight. So, he gave the stranger time to walk that distance, and, then, diving into the wood that lined the road, "stalked" him. From behind a tree he saw the stranger turn and look back, and seeing no one in the road behind him, also leave it and plunge into the woods.

He had not turned toward Bedford; he had turned to the left. Like a runner stealing bases, Jimmie slipped from tree to tree. Ahead of him he heard the stranger trampling upon dead twigs, moving rapidly as one who knew his way. At times through the branches Jimmie could see the broad shoulders of the stranger, and again could follow his progress only by the noise of the crackling twigs. When the noises ceased, Jimmie guessed the stranger had reached the wood road, grass-grown and moss-covered, that led to Middle Patent. So, he ran at right angles until he also reached it, and as now he was close to where it entered the main road, he approached warily. But, he was too late. There was a sound like the whir of a rising partridge, and ahead of him from where it had been hidden, a gray touring-car leaped into the highway. The stranger was at the wheel. Throwing behind it a cloud of dust, the car raced toward Greenwich. Jimmie had time to note only that it bore a Connecticut State license; that in the wheel-ruts the tires printed little V's, like arrow-heads.

For a week Jimmie saw nothing of the spy, but for many hot and dusty miles he stalked arrow-heads. They lured him north, they lured him south, they were stamped in soft asphalt, in mud, dust, and fresh-spread tarvia. Wherever Jimmie walked, arrow-heads ran before. In his sleep as in his copy-book, he saw endless chains of V's. But not once could he catch up with the wheels that printed them. A week later, just at sunset as he passed below Round Hill, he saw the stranger on top of it. On the skyline, in silhouette against the sinking sun, he was as conspicuous as a flagstaff. But to approach him was impossible. For acres Round Hill offered no other cover than stubble. It was as bald as a skull. Until the stranger chose to descend, Jimmie must wait. And the stranger was in no haste. The sun sank and from the west Jimmie saw him turn his face east toward the Sound. A storm was gathering, drops of rain began to splash and as the sky grew black the figure on the hilltop faded into the darkness. And then, at the very spot where Jimmie had last seen it, there suddenly flared two tiny flashes of fire. Jimmie leaped from cover. It was no longer to be endured. The spy was signalling. The time for caution had passed, now was the time to act. Jimmie raced to the top of the hill, and found it empty. He plunged down it, vaulted a stone wall, forced his way through a tangle of saplings, and held his breath to listen. Just beyond him, over a jumble of rocks, a hidden stream was tripping and tumbling. Joyfully, it laughed and gurgled. Jimmie turned hot. It sounded as though from the darkness the spy mocked him. Jimmie shook his fist at the enshrouding darkness. Above the tumult of the coming storm and the tossing tree-tops, he raised his voice.

"You wait!" he shouted. "I'll get you yet! Next time, I'll bring a gun."

Next time, was the next morning. There had been a hawk hovering over the chicken yard, and Jimmie used that fact to explain his borrowing the family shotgun. He loaded it with buckshot, and, in the pocket of his shirt buttoned his license to "hunt, pursue and kill, to take with traps or other devices."

He remembered that Judge Van Vorst had warned him, before he arrested more spies, to come to him for a warrant. But with an impatient shake of the head Jimmie tossed the recollection from him. After what he had seen he could not possibly be again mistaken. He did not need a warrant. What he had seen was his warrant - plus the shotgun.

As a "pathfinder" should, he planned to take up the trail where he had lost it, but, before he reached Round Hill, he found a warmer trail. Before him, stamped clearly in the road still damp from the rain of the night before, two lines of little arrow-heads pointed the way. They were so fresh that at each twist in the road, lest the car should be just beyond him, Jimmie slackened his steps. After half a mile the scent grew hot. The tracks were deeper, the arrow-heads more clearly cut, and Jimmie broke into a run. Then, the arrow-heads swung suddenly to the right, and in a clearing at the edge of a wood, were lost. But the tires had pressed deep into the grass, and just inside the wood, he found the car. It was empty. Jimmie was drawn two ways. Should he seek the spy on the nearest hilltop, or, until the owner returned, wait by the car. Between lying in ambush and action, Jimmie preferred action. But, he did not climb the hill nearest the car; he climbed the hill that overlooked that hill.

Flat on the ground, hidden in the golden-rod he lay motionless. Before him, for fifteen miles stretched hills and tiny valleys. Six miles away to his right rose the stone steeple, and the red roofs of Greenwich. Directly before him were no signs of habitation, only green forests, green fields, gray stone walls, and, where a road ran up-hill, a splash of white, that quivered in the heat. The storm of the night before had washed the air. Each leaf stood by itself. Nothing stirred; and in the glare of the August sun every detail of the landscape was as distinct as those in a colored photograph; and as still.

In his excitement the scout was trembling.

"If he moves," he sighed happily, "I've got him!"

Opposite, across a little valley was the hill at the base of which he had found the car. The slope toward him was bare, but the top was crowned with a thick wood; and along its crest, as though establishing an ancient boundary, ran a stone wall, moss-covered and wrapped in poison-ivy. In places, the branches of the trees, reaching out to the sun, overhung the wall and hid it in black shadows. Jimmie divided the hill into sectors. He began at the right, and slowly followed the wall. With his eyes he took it apart, stone by stone. Had a chipmunk raised his head, Jimmie would have seen him. So, when from the stone wall, like the reflection of the sun upon a window-pane, something flashed, Jimmie knew he had found his spy. A pair of binoculars had betrayed him. Jimmie now saw him clearly. He sat on the ground at the top of the hill opposite, in the deep shadow of an oak, his back against the stone wall. With the binoculars to his eyes he had leaned too far forward, and upon the glass the sun had flashed a warning.

Jimmie appreciated that his attack must be made from the rear. Backward, like a crab he wriggled free of the golden-rod, and hidden by the contour of the hill, raced down it and into the woods on the hill opposite. When he came to within twenty feet of the oak beneath which he had seen the stranger, he stood erect, and as though avoiding a live wire, stepped on tip-toe to the wall. The stranger still sat against it. The binoculars hung from a cord around his neck. Across his knees was spread a map. He was marking it with a pencil, and as he worked, he hummed a tune.

Jimmie knelt, and resting the gun on the top of the wall, covered him.

"Throw up your hands!" he commanded.

The stranger did not start. Except that he raised his eyes he gave no sign that he had heard. His eyes stared across the little sun-filled valley. They were half closed as though in study, as though perplexed by some deep and intricate problem. They appeared to see beyond the sun-filled valley some place of greater moment, some place far distant.

Then the eyes smiled, and slowly, as though his neck were stiff, but still smiling, the stranger turned his head. When he saw the boy, his smile was swept away in waves of surprise, amazement, and disbelief. These were followed instantly by an expression of the most acute alarm. "Don't point that thing at me!" shouted the stranger. "Is it loaded?" With his cheek pressed to the stock and his eye squinted down the length of the brown barrel, Jimmie nodded. The stranger flung up his open palms. They accented his expression of amazed incredulity. He seemed to be exclaiming, "Can such things be?"

"Get up!" commanded Jimmie.

With alacrity the stranger rose.

"Walk over there," ordered the scout. "Walk backward. Stop! Take off those field-glasses and throw them to me." Without removing his eyes from the gun the stranger lifted the binoculars from his neck and tossed them to the stone wall. "See here!" he pleaded, "if you'll only point that damned blunderbuss the other way, you can have the glasses, and my watch, and clothes, and all my money; only don't - "

Jimmie flushed crimson. "You can't bribe me," he growled. At least, he tried to growl, but because his voice was changing, or because he was excited the growl ended in a high squeak. With mortification, Jimmie flushed a deeper crimson. But the stranger was not amused. At Jimmie's words he seemed rather the more amazed.

"I'm not trying to bribe you," he protested. "If you don't want anything, why are you holding me up?"

"I'm not," returned Jimmie, "I'm arresting you!"

The stranger laughed with relief. Again his eyes smiled. "Oh," he cried, "I see! Have I been trespassing?"

With a glance Jimmie measured the distance between himself and the stranger. Reassured, he lifted one leg after the other over the wall. "If you try to rush me," he warned, "I'll shoot you full of buckshot."

The stranger took a hasty step BACKWARD. "Don't worry about that," he exclaimed. "I'll not rush you. Why am I arrested?"

Hugging the shotgun with his left arm, Jimmie stopped and lifted the binoculars. He gave them a swift glance, slung them over his shoulder, and again clutched his weapon. His expression was now stern and menacing.

"The name on them" he accused, "is 'Weiss, Berlin.' Is that your name?" The stranger smiled, but corrected himself, and replied gravely, "That's the name of the firm that makes them."

Jimmie exclaimed in triumph. "Hah!" he cried, "made in Germany!"

The stranger shook his head.

"I don't understand," he said. "Where WOULD a Weiss glass be made?" With polite insistence he repeated, "Would you mind telling me why I am arrested, and who you might happen to be?"

Jimmie did not answer. Again he stooped and picked

up the map, and as he did so, for the first time the face of the stranger showed that he was annoyed. Jimmie was not at home with maps. They told him nothing. But the penciled notes on this one made easy reading. At his first glance he saw, "Correct range, 1,800 yards"; "this stream not fordable"; "slope of hill 15 degrees inaccessible for artillery." "Wire entanglements here"; "forage for five squadrons."

Jimmie's eyes flashed. He shoved the map inside his shirt, and with the gun motioned toward the base of the hill. "Keep forty feet ahead of me," he commanded, "and walk to your car." The stranger did not seem to hear him. He spoke with irritation.

"I suppose," he said, "I'll have to explain to you about that map."

"Not to me, you won't," declared his captor. "You're going to drive straight to Judge Van Vorst's, and explain to HIM!"

The stranger tossed his arms even higher. "Thank God!" he exclaimed gratefully.

With his prisoner Jimmie encountered no further trouble. He made a willing captive. And if in covering the five miles to Judge Van Vorst's he exceeded the speed limit, the fact that from the rear seat Jimmie held the shotgun against the base of his skull was an extenuating circumstance.

They arrived in the nick of time. In his own car young Van Vorst and a bag of golf clubs were just drawing away from the house. Seeing the car climbing the steep driveway that for a half-mile led from his lodge to his front door, and seeing Jimmie standing in the tonneau brandishing a gun, the Judge hastily descended. The sight of the spy hunter filled him with misgiving, but the sight of him gave Jimmie sweet relief. Arresting German spies for a small boy is no easy task. For Jimmie the strain was great. And now that he knew he had successfully delivered him into the hands of the law, Jimmie's heart rose with happiness. The added presence of a butler of magnificent bearing and of an athletic looking chauffeur increased his sense of security. Their presence seemed to afford a feeling of security to the prisoner also. As he brought the car to a halt, he breathed a sigh. It was a sigh of deep relief.

Jimmie fell from the tonneau. In concealing his sense of triumph, he was not entirety successful.

"I got him!" he cried. "I didn't make no mistake about THIS one!"

"What one?" demanded Van Vorst.

Jimmie pointed dramatically at his prisoner. With an anxious expression the stranger was tenderly fingering the back of his head. He seemed to wish to assure himself that it was still there.

"THAT one!" cried Jimmie. "He's a German spy!"

The patience of Judge Van Vorst fell from him. In his exclamation was indignation, anger, reproach.

"Jimmie!" he cried.

Jimmie thrust into his hand the map. It was his "Exhibit A." "Look what he's wrote," commanded the scout. "It's all military words. And these are his glasses. I took 'em off him. They're made in GERMANY! I been stalking him for a week. He's a spy!"

When Jimmie thrust the map before his face, Van Vorst had glanced at it. Then he regarded it more closely. As he raised his eyes they showed that he was puzzled.

But he greeted the prisoner politely.

"I'm extremely sorry you've been annoyed," he said. "I'm only glad it's no worse. He might have shot you. He's mad over the idea that every stranger he sees - "

The prisoner quickly interrupted.

"Please!" he begged, "Don't blame the boy. He behaved extremely well. Might I speak with you - ALONE?" he asked.

Judge Van Vorst led the way across the terrace, and to the smoking-room, that served also as his office, and closed the door. The stranger walked directly to the mantelpiece and put his finger on a gold cup.

"I saw your mare win that at Belmont Park," he said. "She must have been a great loss to you?"

"She was," said Van Vorst. "The week before she broke her back, I refused three thousand for her. Will you have a cigarette?"

The stranger waved aside the cigarettes.

"I brought you inside," he said, "because I didn't want your servants to hear; and because I don't want to hurt that boy's feelings. He's a fine boy; and he's a damned clever scout. I knew he was following me and I threw him off twice, but to-day he caught me fair. If I really had been a German spy, I couldn't have got away from him. And I want him to think he has captured a German spy. Because he deserves just as much credit as though he had, and because it's best he shouldn't know whom he DID capture."

Van Vorst pointed to the map. "My bet is," he said, "that you're an officer of the State militia, taking notes for the fall manoeuvres. Am I right?"

The stranger smiled in approval, but shook his head.

"You're warm," he said, "but it's more serious than manoeuvres. It's the Real Thing." From his pocketbook he took a visiting card and laid it on the table. "I'm 'Sherry' McCoy," he said, "Captain of Artillery in the United States Army." He nodded to the hand telephone on the table.

"You can call up Governor's Island and get General Wood or his aide, Captain Dorey, on the phone. They sent me here. Ask THEM. I'm not picking out gun sites for the Germans; I'm picking out positions of defense for Americans when the Germans come!"

Van Vorst laughed derisively.

"My word!" he exclaimed. "You're as bad as Jimmie!"

Captain McCoy regarded him with disfavor.

"And you, sir," he retorted, "are as bad as ninety million other Americans. You WON'T believe! When the Germans are shelling this hill, when they're taking your hunters to pull their cook-wagons, maybe, you'll believe THEN."

"Are you serious?" demanded Van Vorst. "And you an army officer?"

"That's why I am serious," returned McCoy. "WE know. But when we try to prepare for what is coming, we must do it secretly - in underhand ways, for fear the newspapers will get hold of it and ridicule us, and accuse us of trying to drag the country into war. That's why we have to prepare under cover. That's why I've had to skulk around these hills like a chicken thief. And," he added sharply, "that's why that boy must not know who I am. If he does, the General Staff will get a calling down at Washington, and I'll have my ears boxed."

Van Vorst moved to the door.

"He will never learn the truth from me," he said. "For I will tell him you are to be shot at sunrise."

"Good!" laughed the Captain. "And tell me his name. If ever we fight over Westchester County, I want that lad for my chief of scouts. And give him this. Tell him to buy a new scout uniform. Tell him it comes from you."

But no money could reconcile Jimmie to the sentence imposed upon his captive. He received the news with a howl of anguish. "You mustn't," he begged; "I never knowed you'd shoot him! I wouldn't have caught him, if I'd knowed that. I couldn't sleep if I thought he was going to be shot at sunrise." At the prospect of unending nightmares Jimmie's voice shook with terror. "Make it for twenty years," he begged. "Make it for ten," he coaxed, "but, please, promise you won't shoot him."

When Van Vorst returned to Captain McCoy, he was smiling, and the butler who followed, bearing a tray and tinkling glasses, was trying not to smile.

"I gave Jimmie your ten dollars," said Van Vorst, "and made it twenty, and he has gone home. You will be glad to hear that he begged me to spare your life, and that your sentence has been commuted to twenty years in a fortress. I drink to your good fortune."

"No!" protested Captain McCoy, "We will drink to Jimmie!"

When Captain McCoy had driven away, and his own car and the golf clubs had again been brought to the steps, Judge Van Vorst once more attempted to depart; but he was again delayed.

Other visitors were arriving.

Up the driveway a touring-car approached, and though it limped on a flat tire, it approached at reckless speed. The two men in the front seat were white with dust; their faces, masked by automobile glasses, were indistinguishable. As though preparing for an immediate exit, the car swung in a circle until its nose pointed down the driveway up which it had just come. Raising his silk mask the one beside the driver shouted at Judge Van Vorst. His throat was parched, his voice was hoarse and hot with anger.

"A gray touring-car," he shouted. "It stopped here. We saw it from that hill. Then the damn tire burst, and we lost our way. Where did he go?"

"Who?" demanded Van Vorst, stiffly, "Captain McCoy?"

The man exploded with an oath. The driver with a shove of his elbow, silenced him.

"Yes, Captain McCoy," assented the driver eagerly. "Which way did he go?"

"To New York," said Van Vorst.

The driver shrieked at his companion.

"Then, he's doubled back," he cried. "He's gone to New Haven." He stooped and threw in the clutch. The car lurched forward.

A cold terror swept young Van Vorst.

"What do you want with him?" he called "Who are you?"

Over one shoulder the masked face glared at him. Above the roar of the car the words of the driver were flung back. "We're Secret Service from Washington," he shouted. "He's from their embassy. He's a German spy!"

Leaping and throbbing at sixty miles an hour, the car vanished in a curtain of white, whirling dust.

Chapter 9.

THE CARD-SHARP

I had looked forward to spending Christmas with some people in Suffolk, and every one in London assured me that at their house there would be the kind of a Christmas house party you hear about but see only in the illustrated Christmas numbers. They promised mistletoe, snapdragon, and Sir Roger de Coverley. On Christmas morning we would walk to church, after luncheon we would shoot, after dinner we would eat plum pudding floating in blazing brandy, dance with the servants, and listen to the waits singing "God rest you, merry gentlemen, let nothing you dismay."

To a lone American bachelor stranded in London it sounded fine. And in my gratitude I had already shipped to my hostess, for her children, of whose age, number, and sex I was ignorant, half of Gamage's dolls, skees, and cricket bats, and those crackers that, when you pull them, sometimes explode. But it was not to be. Most inconsiderately my wealthiest patient gained sufficient courage to consent to an operation, and in all New York would permit no one to lay violent hands upon him save myself. By cable I advised postponement. Having lived in lawful harmony with his appendix for fifty years, I thought, for one week longer he might safely maintain the status quo. But his cable in reply was an ultimatum. So, on Christmas eve, instead of Hallam Hall and a Yule log, I was in a gale plunging and pitching off the coast of Ireland, and the only log on board was the one the captain kept to himself.

I sat in the smoking-room, depressed and cross, and it must have been on the principle that misery loves company that I foregathered with Talbot, or rather that Talbot foregathered with me. Certainty, under happier conditions and in haunts of men more crowded, the open-faced manner in which he forced himself upon me would have put me on my guard. But, either out of deference to the holiday spirit, as manifested in the fictitious gayety of our few fellow-passengers, or because the young man in a knowing, impertinent way was most amusing, I listened to him from dinner time until midnight, when the chief officer, hung with snow and icicles, was blown in from the deck and wished all a merry Christmas.

Even after they unmasked Talbot I had neither the heart nor the inclination to turn him down. Indeed, had not some of the passengers testified that I belonged to a different profession, the smoking-room crowd would have quarantined me as his accomplice. On the first night I met him I was not certain whether he was English or giving an imitation. All the outward and visible signs were English, but he told me that, though he had been educated at Oxford and since then had spent most of his years in India, playing polo, he was an American. He seemed to have spent much time, and according to himself much money, at the French watering-places and on the Riviera. I felt sure that it was in France I had already seen him, but where I could not recall. He was hard to place. Of people at home and in London well worth knowing he talked glibly, but in speaking of them he made several slips. It was his taking the trouble to cover up the slips that first made me wonder if his talking about himself was not mere vanity, but had some special object. I felt he was presenting letters of introduction in order that later he might ask a favor. Whether he was leading up to an immediate loan, or in New York would ask for a card to a club, or an introduction to a banker, I could not tell. But in forcing himself upon me, except in self-interest, I could think of no other motive. The next evening I discovered the motive.

He was in the smoking-room playing solitaire, and at once I recalled that it was at Aix-les-Bains I had first seen him, and that he held a bank at baccarat. When he asked me to sit down I said: "I saw you last summer at Aix-les-Bains."

His eyes fell to the pack in his hands and apparently searched it for some particular card.

"What was I doing?" he asked.

"Dealing baccarat at the Casino des Fleurs."

With obvious relief he laughed.

"Oh, yes," he assented; "jolly place, Aix. But I lost a pot of money there. I'm a rotten hand at cards. Can't win, and can't leave 'em alone." As though for this weakness, so frankly confessed, he begged me to excuse him, he smiled appealingly. "Poker, bridge, chemin de fer, I like 'em all," he rattled on, "but they don't like me. So I stick to solitaire. It's dull, but cheap." He shuffled the cards clumsily. As though making conversation, he asked: "You care for cards yourself?"

I told him truthfully I did not know the difference between a club and a spade and had no curiosity to learn. At this, when he found he had been wasting time on me, I expected him to show some sign of annoyance, even of irritation, but his disappointment struck far deeper. As though I had hurt him physically, he shut his eyes, and when again he opened them I saw in them distress. For the moment I believe of my presence he was utterly unconscious. His hands lay idle upon the table; like a man facing a crisis, he stared before him. Quite improperly, I felt sorry for him. In me he thought he had found a victim; and that the loss of the few dollars he might have won should so deeply disturb him showed his need was great. Almost at once he abandoned me and I went on deck. When I returned an hour later to the smoking-room he was deep in a game of poker.

As I passed he hailed me gayly.

"Don't scold, now," he laughed; "you know I can't keep away from it."

From his manner those at the table might have supposed we were friends of long and happy companionship. I stopped behind his chair, but he thought I had passed, and in reply to one of the players answered: "Known him for years; he's set me right many a time. When I broke my right femur 'chasin,' he got me back in the saddle in six weeks. All my people swear by him."

One of the players smiled up at me, and Talbot turned.

But his eyes met mine with perfect serenity. He even held up his cards for me to see. "What would you draw?" he asked.

His audacity so astonished me that in silence I could only stare at him and walk on.

When on deck he met me he was not even apologetic. Instead, as though we were partners in crime, he chuckled delightedly.

"Sorry," he said. "Had to do it. They weren't very keen at my taking a hand, so I had to use your name. But I'm all right now," he assured me. "They think you vouched for me, and to-night they're going to raise the limit. I've convinced them I'm an easy mark."

"And I take it you are not," I said stiffly.

He considered this unworthy of an answer and only smiled. Then the smile died, and again in his eyes I saw distress, infinite weariness, and fear.

As though his thoughts drove him to seek protection, he came closer.

"I'm 'in bad,' doctor," he said. His voice was frightened, bewildered, like that of a child. "I can't sleep; nerves all on the loose. I don't think straight. I hear voices, and no one around. I hear knockings at the door, and when I open it, no one there. If I don't keep fit I can't work, and this trip I got to make expenses. You couldn't help me, could you - couldn't give me something to keep my head straight?"

The need of my keeping his head straight that he might

the easier rob our fellow-passengers raised a pretty question of ethics. I meanly dodged it. I told him professional etiquette required I should leave him to the ship's surgeon.

"But I don't know HIM," he protested.

Mindful of the use he had made of my name, I objected strenuously:

"Well, you certainly don't know me."

My resentment obviously puzzled him.

"I know who you ARE," he returned. "You and I - "With a deprecatory gesture, as though good taste forbade him saying who we were, he stopped. "But the ship's surgeon!" he protested, "he's an awful bounder! Besides," he added quite simply, "he's watching me."

"As a doctor," I asked, "or watching you play cards?"

"Play cards," the young man answered. "I'm afraid he was ship's surgeon on the P. & O. I came home on. There was trouble that voyage, and I fancy he remembers me."

His confidences were becoming a nuisance.

"But you mustn't tell me that," I protested. "I can't have you making trouble on this ship, too. How do you know I won't go straight from here to the captain?"

As though the suggestion greatly entertained him, he laughed.

He made a mock obeisance.

"I claim the seal of your profession," he said. "Nonsense," I retorted. "It's a professional secret that your nerves are out of hand, but that you are a card-sharp is NOT. Don't mix me up with a priest."

For a moment Talbot, as though fearing he had gone too far, looked at me sharply; he bit his lower lip and frowned.

"I got to make expenses," he muttered. "And, besides, all card games are games of chance, and a card-sharp is one of the chances. Anyway," he repeated, as though disposing of all argument, "I got to make expenses."

After dinner, when I came to the smoking-room, the poker party sat waiting, and one of them asked if I knew where they could find "my friend." I should have said then that Talbot was a steamer acquaintance only; but I hate a row, and I let the chance pass.

"We want to give him his revenge," one of them volunteered.

"He's losing, then?" I asked.

The man chuckled complacently.

"The only loser," he said.

"I wouldn't worry," I advised. "He'll come for his revenge."

That night after I had turned in he knocked at my door. I switched on the lights and saw him standing at the foot of my berth. I saw also that with difficulty he was holding himself in hand.

"I'm scared," he stammered, "scared!"

I wrote out a requisition on the surgeon for a sleeping-potion and sent it to him by the steward, giving the man to understand I wanted it for myself. Uninvited, Talbot had seated himself on the sofa. His eyes were closed, and as though he were cold he was shivering and hugging himself in his arms.

"Have you been drinking?" I asked.

In surprise he opened his eyes.

"I can't drink," he answered simply. "It's nerves and worry. I'm tired."

He relaxed against the cushions; his arms fell heavily at his sides; the fingers lay open.

"God," he whispered, "how tired I am!"

In spite of his tan - and certainly he had led the out-of-door life - his face showed white. For the moment he looked old, worn, finished.

"They're crowdin' me," the boy whispered. "They're always crowdin' me." His voice was querulous, uncomprehending, like that of a child complaining of something beyond his experience. "I can't remember when they haven't been crowdin' me. Movin' me on, you understand? Always movin' me on. Moved me out of India, then Cairo, then they closed Paris, and now they've shut me out of London. I opened a club there, very quiet, very exclusive, smart neighborhood, too - a flat in Berkeley Street - roulette and chemin de fer. I think it was my valet sold me out; anyway, they came in and took us all to Bow Street. So I've plunged on this. It's my last chance!"

"This trip?"

"No; my family in New York. Haven't seen 'em in ten years. They paid me to live abroad. I'm gambling on THEM; gambling on their takin' me back. I'm coming home as the Prodigal Son, tired of filling my belly with the husks that the swine do eat; reformed character, repentant and all that; want to follow the straight and narrow; and they'll kill the fatted calf." He laughed sardonically. "Like hell they will! They'd rather see ME killed."

It seemed to me, if he wished his family to believe he were returning repentant, his course in the smoking-room would not help to reassure them. I suggested as much.

"If you get into 'trouble,' as you call it," I said, "and they send a wireless to the police to be at the wharf, your people would hardly - "

"I know," he interrupted; "but I got to chance that. I GOT to make enough to go on with - until I see my family."

"If they won't see you?" I asked. "What then?"

He shrugged his shoulders and sighed lightly, almost with relief, as though for him the prospect held no terror.

"Then it's 'Good-night, nurse,'" he said. "And I won't be a bother to anybody any more."

I told him his nerves were talking, and talking rot, and I gave him the sleeping-draft and sent him to bed.

It was not until after luncheon the next day when he made his first appearance on deck that I again saw my patient. He was once more a healthy picture of a young Englishman of leisure; keen, smart, and fit; ready for any exercise or sport. The particular sport at which he was so expert I asked him to avoid.

"Can't be done!" he assured me. "I'm the loser, and we dock to-morrow morning. So tonight I've got to make my killing."

It was the others who made the killing.

I came into the smoking-room about nine o'clock. Talbot alone was seated. The others were on their feet, and behind them in a wider semicircle were passengers, the smoking-room stewards and the ship's purser.

Talbot sat with his back against the bulkhead, his hands in the pockets of his dinner coat; from the corner of his mouth his long cigarette-holder was cocked at an impudent angle. There was a tumult of angry voices, and the eyes of all were turned upon him. Outwardly at least he met them with complete indifference. The voice of one of my countrymen, a noisy pest named Smedburg, was raised in excited accusation.

"When the ship's surgeon first met you," he cried, "you called yourself Lord Ridley."

"I'll call myself anything I jolly well like," returned Talbot. "If I choose to dodge reporters, that's my pidgin. I don't have to give my name to every meddling busybody that - "

"You'll give it to the police, all right," chortled Mr. Smedburg. In the confident, bullying tones of the man who knows the crowd is with him, he shouted: "And in the meantime you'll keep out of this smoking-room!"

The chorus of assent was unanimous. It could not be disregarded. Talbot rose and with fastidious concern brushed the cigarette ashes from his sleeve. As he moved toward the door he called back: "Only too delighted to keep out. The crowd in this room makes a gentleman feel lonely."

But he was not to escape with the last word.

His prosecutor pointed his finger at him.

"And the next time you take the name of Adolph Meyer," he shouted, "make sure first he hasn't a friend on board; some one to protect him from sharpers and swindlers - "

Talbot turned savagely and then shrugged his shoulders.

"Oh, go to the devil!" he called, and walked out into the night.

The purser was standing at my side and, catching my eye, shook his head.

"Bad business," he exclaimed.

"What happened?" I asked.

"I'm told they caught him dealing from the wrong end of the pack," he said. "I understand they suspected him from the first - seems our surgeon recognized him - and to-night they had outsiders watching him. The outsiders claim they saw him slip himself an ace from the bottom of the pack. It's a pity! He's a nice-looking lad."

I asked what the excited Smedburg had meant by telling Talbot not to call himself Meyer.

"They accused him of travelling under a false name," explained the purser, "and he told 'em he did it to dodge the ship's news reporters. Then he said he really was a brother of Adolph Meyer, the banker; but it seems Smedburg is a friend of Meyer's, and he called him hard! It was a silly ass thing to do," protested the purser. "Everybody knows Meyer hasn't a brother, and if he hadn't made THAT break he might have got away with the other one. But now this Smedburg is going to wireless ahead to Mr. Meyer and to the police."

"Has he no other way of spending his money?" I asked.

"He's a confounded nuisance!" growled the purser. "He wants to show us he knows Adolph Meyer; wants to put Meyer under an obligation. It means a scene on the wharf, and newspaper talk; and," he added with disgust, "these smoking-room rows never helped any line."

I went in search of Talbot; partly because I knew he was on the verge of a collapse, partly, as I frankly admitted to myself, because I was sorry the young man had come to grief. I searched the snow-swept decks, and then, after threading my way through faintly lit tunnels, I knocked at his cabin. The sound of his voice gave me a distinct feeling of relief. But he would not admit me. Through the closed door he declared he was "all right," wanted no medical advice, and asked only to resume the sleep he claimed I had broken. I left him, not without uneasiness, and the next morning the sight of him still in the flesh was a genuine thrill. I found him walking the deck carrying himself nonchalantly and trying to appear unconscious of the glances - amused, contemptuous, hostile - that were turned toward him. He would have passed me without speaking, but I took his arm and led him to the rail. We had long passed quarantine and a convoy of tugs were butting us into the dock.

"What are you going to do?" I asked.

"Doesn't depend on me," he said. "Depends on Smedburg. He's a busy little body!"

The boy wanted me to think him unconcerned, but beneath the flippancy I saw the nerves jerking. Then quite simply he began to tell me. He spoke in a low, even monotone, dispassionately, as though for him the incident no longer was of interest.

"They were watching me," he said. "But I knew they were, and besides, no matter how close they watched I could have done what they said I did and they'd never have seen it. But I didn't."

My scepticism must have been obvious, for he shook his head.

"I didn't!" he repeated stubbornly. "I didn't have to! I was playing in luck - wonderful luck - sheer, dumb luck. I couldn't HELP winning. But because I was winning and because they were watching, I was careful not to win on my own deal. I laid down, or played to lose. It was the cards they GAVE me I won with. And when they jumped me I told 'em that. I could have proved it if they'd listened. But they were all up in the air, shouting and spitting at me. They believed what they wanted to believe; they didn't want the facts."

It may have been credulous of me, but I felt the boy was telling the truth, and I was deeply sorry he had not stuck to it. So, rather harshly, I said:

"They didn't want you to tell them you were a brother to Adolph Meyer, either. Why did you think you could get away with anything like that?"

Talbot did not answer.

"Why?" I insisted.

The boy laughed impudently.

"How the devil was I to know he hadn't a brother?" he protested. "It was a good name, and he's a Jew, and two of the six who were in the game are Jews. You know how they stick together. I thought they might stick by me."

"But you," I retorted impatiently, "are not a Jew!"

"I am not," said Talbot, "but I've often SAID I was. It's helped - lots of times. If I'd told you my name was Cohen, or Selinsky, or Meyer, instead of Craig Talbot,

YOU'D have thought I was a Jew." He smiled and turned his face toward me. As though furnishing a description for the police, he began to enumerate:

"Hair, dark and curly; eyes, poppy; lips, full; nose, Roman or Hebraic, according to taste. Do you see?"

He shrugged his shoulders.

"But it didn't work," he concluded. "I picked the wrong Jew."

His face grew serious. "Do you suppose that Smedburg person has wirelessed that banker?"

I told him I was afraid he had already sent the message.

"And what will Meyer do?" he asked. "Will he drop it or make a fuss? What sort is he?"

Briefly I described Adolph Meyer. I explained him as the richest Hebrew in New York; given to charity, to philanthropy, to the betterment of his own race.

"Then maybe," cried Talbot hopefully, "he won't make a row, and my family won't hear of it!"

He drew a quick breath of relief. As though a burden had been lifted, his shoulders straightened.

And then suddenly, harshly, in open panic, he exclaimed aloud:

"Look!" he whispered. "There, at the end of the wharf - the little Jew in furs!"

I followed the direction of his eyes. Below us on the dock, protected by two obvious members of the strong-arm squad, the great banker, philanthropist, and Hebrew, Adolph Meyer, was waiting.

We were so close that I could read his face. It was stern, set; the face of a man intent upon his duty, unrelenting. Without question, of a bad business Mr. Smedburg had made the worst. I turned to speak to Talbot and found him gone.

His silent slipping away filled me with alarm. I fought against a growing fear. How many minutes I searched for him I do not know. It seemed many hours. His cabin, where first I sought him, was empty and dismantled, and by that I was reminded that if for any desperate purpose Talbot were seeking to conceal himself there now were hundreds of other empty, dismantled cabins in which he might hide. To my inquiries no one gave heed. In the confusion of departure no one had observed him; no one was in a humor to seek him out; the passengers were pressing to the gangway, the stewards concerned only in counting their tips. From deck to deck, down lane after lane of the great floating village, I raced blindly, peering into half-opened doors, pushing through groups of men, pursuing some one in the distance who appeared to be the man I sought, only to find he was unknown to me. When I returned to the gangway the last of the passengers was leaving it.

I was about to follow to seek for Talbot in the customs shed when a white-faced steward touched my sleeve. Before he spoke his look told me why I was wanted.

" The ship's surgeon , sir , " he stammered, "asks you

please to hurry to the sick-bay. A passenger has shot himself!"

On the bed, propped up by pillows, young Talbot, with glazed, shocked eyes, stared at me. His shirt had been cut away; his chest lay bare. Against his left shoulder the doctor pressed a tiny sponge which quickly darkened.

I must have exclaimed aloud, for the doctor turned his eyes.

"It was HE sent for you," he said, "but he doesn't need you. Fortunately, he's a damned bad shot!"

The boy's eyes opened wearily; before we could prevent it he spoke.

"I was so tired," he whispered. "Always moving me on. I was so tired!"

Behind me came heavy footsteps, and though with my arm I tried to bar them out, the two detectives pushed into the doorway. They shoved me to one side and through the passage made for him came the Jew in the sable coat, Mr. Adolph Meyer.

For an instant the little great man stood with wide, owl-like eyes, staring at the face on the pillow.

Then he sank softly to his knees. In both his hands he caught the hand of the card-sharp.

"Heine!" he begged. "Don't you know me? It is your brother Adolph; your little brother Adolph!"

www.ingramcontent.com/pod-product-compliance
Lightning Source LLC
Chambersburg PA
CBHW030122180626

46812CB00002B/523